PRETTY KINGS V

THE CLASH

T. STYLES

By T. STYLES

ARE YOU ON OUR EMAIL LIST?

SIGN UP ON OUR WEBSITE

www.thecartelpublications.com

CHECK OUT OTHER TITLES BY THE CARTEL PUBLICATIONS

By T. STYLES

4

SILENCE OF THE NINE II: LET THERE BE BLOOD
SILENCE OF THE NINE III
PRISON THRONE
GOON
HOETIC JUSTICE
AND THEY CALL ME GOD
THE UNGRATEFUL BASTARDS
LIPSTICK DOM (LGBTQ+)
A SCHOOL OF DOLLS (LGBTQ+)
SKEEZERS
SKEEZERS 2
YOU KISSED ME NOW I OWN YOU
NEFARIOUS
REDBONE 3: THE RISE OF THE FOLD
THE FOLD
CLOWN NIGGAS
THE ONE YOU SHOULDN'T TRUST
COLD AS ICE
THE WHORE THE WIND BLEW MY WAY
SHE BRINGS THE WORST KIND
THE HOUSE THAT CRACK BUILT
THE HOUSE THAT CRACK BUILT 2: RUSSO & AMINA
THE HOUSE THAT CRACK BUILT 3: REGGIE & TAMIKA
THE HOUSE THAT CRACK BUILT 4: REGGIE & AMINA
LEVEL UP (LGBTQ+)
VILLAINS: IT'S SAVAGE SEASON
GAY FOR MY BAE (LGBTQ+)
WAR
WAR 2
WAR 3
WAR 4
WAR 5
WAR 6
WAR 7
MADJESTY VS. JAYDEN: SHORT STORY
YOU LEFT ME NO CHOICE
TRUCE: A WAR SAGA (WAR 8)
TRUCE 2: THE WAR OF THE LOU'S (WAR 9)
AN ACE AND WALID VERY, VERY BAD CHRISTMAS (WAR 10)
TRUCE 3: SINS OF THE FATHERS (WAR 11)
TRUCE 4: THE FINALE (WAR 12)
ASK THE STREETS FOR MERCY
TREASON
TREASON 2
HERSBAND MATERIAL 2 (LGBTQ+)
THE GODS OF EVERYTHING ELSE (WAR 13)
THE GODS OF EVERYTHING ELSE 2 (WAR 14)
TREASON 3
AN UGLY GIRL'S DIARY
THE GODS OF EVERYTHING ELSE 3 (WAR 15)
AN UGLY GIRL'S DIARY 2
KING DOM (LGBTQ+)
THE GODS OF EVERYTHING ELSE 4 (WAR 16)
RAUNCHY: THE MONSTERS WHO RAISED HARMONY
AN UGLY GIRL'S DIARY 3

PRETTY KINGS 5

WWW.THECARTELPUBLICATIONS.COM

By T. STYLES

PRETTY KINGS 5

By

T. STYLES

Library of Congress Control Number:

ISBN 13: 9781948373951

Cover Design: Book Slut Girl

First Edition

Printed in the United States of America

By T. STYLES

What up Fam,

I hope and pray my little love note finds you at your best! We having a really crazy summer so far with the heat being on HELL and with it being an election year. It's not missed on me that the 2 probably connect. ☺ So stay cool any way you can and don't forget to vote!

Now that the PSA is out the way...PRETTY KINGS 5! Babydoll...This book had me in a chokehold from the time I opened it up to the very last word! I finished it in one sitting and almost threw my laptop across the room twice! It really felt good catching up with characters I love. Before the WAR series, this was my favorite family and I realized I missed Bambi and them! T. Styles threw me for a couple loops and I'm positive, she's gonna get y'all caught up too, so be prepared!

Now, let's shift our focus and keep in line with tradition. In this novel, we want to give love to,

JACOBY JONES

Jacoby Rashi'd Jones was a Superbowl Champion wide receiver and the best return specialist that the Baltimore Ravens ever had! Jacoby Jones played in the league eight years for four different teams and left us with some amazing highlights and end zone dances before signing a one-day contract with the Baltimore Ravens to retire as a part of the team in 2017. Jacoby recently passed away soon after his 40th birthday and he will be heavily missed. May his family be comforted by all the love being expressed since his passing and may this legend truly rest in peace. #12

Aight now, I've kept you from getting this work long enough! Jump into it and I'll catch you in the next one!

Love & Light!

C. Wash
Vice President
The Cartel Publications
www.thecartelpublications.com
www.facebook.com/authortstyles
www.facebook.com/Publishercwash
Instagram: Publishercwash
Instagram: Authortstyles

www.twitter.com/cartelbooks

www.facebook.com/cartelpublications

www.theelitewritersacademy.com

Follow us on IG: Cartelpublications

Follow our Movies on IG: Cartelurbancinema

#CartelPublications

#UrbanFiction

#PrayForCece

#RIPJacobyJones

#PRETTYKINGS5

By T. STYLES

PROLOGUE
PRESENT DAY

*T*he rain fell heavy, throwing D.C. in a watery haze. The relentless downpour beat bricks on the roof of Mystique's, a rundown, almost-empty diner, where neon lights flickered, casting eerie reflections on the wet pavement below.

It was mostly empty but not for long.

And then...

A sleek, black luxury car pulled up to the curb. The engine purred to a stop, and the headlights cut out, pushing the street back into dark shadows. Within moments, the door opened, and fine ass Race Kennedy stepped out. Her long black hair ran down the middle of her back, and the tight blue jeans she wore accentuated her curves. But being a fashion icon was the least of her concerns as the waist-length leather jacket she bodied hid the .45 tucked on her hip. On God her movement was deliberate and tense as she glanced around, her eyes sharp and ready. Whoever wanted smoke would catch a bullet if they desired.

Walking around the perimeter of the car, she hesitated for a moment. Her expression peered beyond the diner, deep into the distance. Her breath visible in the cold air, she knocked on the car's door. "We good."

With the okay given, Denim Kennedy exited, her expression mirroring Race's tension. Something was about to pop off, and it was obvious that they were ready for whatever. The red tights and black top she donned under her white raincoat were stylish but functional. She was sexy, even during the serious situation as she tossed her blue locs over her shoulder. Peering inside the car she said, "Looks clear to me too."

And so another figure was allowed to emerge.

It was Bambi Kennedy.

The baddest bitch herself.

The black catsuit she wore, and the brown leather jacket wrapped her body up like a gift and concealed the two hammers on her hip, held in place by a Gucci belt. She was soaking wet despite the brief exposure to the rain, indicating that something happened someplace else.

"Come on, let's go!" Race huffed; her hand close to her weapon as she watched her sister scan the perimeter of the diner a bit longer. "Bambi, I hope you know what you're doing."

"Name a time where that wasn't the case," Bambi said. "I'll wait."

Race couldn't.

Bambi nodded, and the sisters strolled in silent coordination, their bond and shared purpose evident in their synchronized steps.

Just as Denim reached the door, Bambi's eyes darted around once more before hurrying inside the diner.

A small bell above the door chimed softly. Inside, red and gold were the dominant colors. If blood poured on the floor with a slight squint, you might miss it because it would blend in nicely. This made it the perfect location. As the beautiful criminals made entry, a young black couple posted up doing nothing, looked their way.

"I thought we had the whole place," Race said.

"We do," Bambi responded.

Bambi nodded at Race, issuing a silent order. Reading her mind, Race moved toward the couple, a flash of her gun shocking them as she dug into her pocket jacket, removing a wad of money instead of the handle of her gun.

They were lucky.

For now.

"It's like this…find someplace else to fucking eat."

"But we waiting on our ride," the woman said, scratching between the rows of her braids. She raised her strawberry shake to show her the frothy mess as if Race gave a fuck. "And I was sipping my drink. So nah, we good."

Thinking she got out on Race, her nigga chuckled…and then he saw something she didn't.

Danger.

Race leaned down. "If you don't get the fuck out of here, you gonna be sucking back blood." Now the weapon hung in her hand. "Is that drink that good?"

"We'll take the money."

Denim opened the door.

With five hundred dollars and their lives, they scurried out, the bell bidding them good fucking riddance.

With them gone, Bambi and her sisters slid into a corner red leather booth. Bambi sat alone on her side, while Denim and Race posted across from her. Nobody was comfortable but Bambi appeared confident as her eyes rested firmly on the door.

Shit felt heavy.

Like everything was on the line, because it was.

When Bambi's beautiful brown skin shimmered in the harsh white lights from the outside, Race nodded. "They here?"

Bambi nodded. "Get ready."

CHAPTER ONE
BAMBI
WEEKS EARLIER

I wake up before dawn, blinded a little from light filtering through a small slit between the heavy royal blue curtains. Kevin is beside me, his breathing steady, deep and peaceful. I watch him for a moment, feeling a strange mixture of love and hate for reasons I can't be sure. Quietly, I slip out of bed, determined not to wake him. If I did, he would want to fuck all over again, and as hard as I tried, I could never keep up with him anymore.

He didn't care if I was interested in sex just because. Pussy was his answer for everything.

Problems with the connect delaying our coke shipment? He wanted pussy.

Beef with his brothers? He wanted pussy.

But there was something more driving him. Something I knew that he didn't. For him, fucking me was a way to keep me in line. To control me. So I let him believe he had the upper hand just to keep the peace. Besides I was making money and still the head of a thriving drug empire. And I love that shit.

But he was talking crazy again. Hollering about he wanted out and because of it he was drying my box up.

Naked, I pushed the sheets back and tiptoed to the floor-to-ceiling window. Shoving the curtains gently, I glanced out at our land. From my view, I could see the front of our mansion in Maryland, which was tucked away, nestled in a secluded area surrounded by dense trees. Our off-white brick mansion loomed large, with a circular driveway winding its way through the shadowy woods. From this view, I could see an enemy coming from miles away right before they ate a bullet. Even now, with the mist clinging to the ground, making everything look slightly eerie in the early morning light, if a nigga tried me, even from this distance it would be off with his head.

"Come back to bed," Kevin said, rubbing his chiseled muscular chest.

How did he know when I was away from his grasp? Could he feel my absence?

After all these years, he was still fine, and the print rising from his white boxers let me know he was already frozen for me. What was it about men that caused them to look better with age?

Me and my girls always felt like we had to stay one step on top of our looks to prevent age from coming too soon, but him...he was always fucking right.

I leaned against the wall by the window. "No," I smiled.

He tossed the expensive white sheet and blankets further away from where I just laid. A playful grin covered his expression. "Get over here. Now. Or do you want me to come get you?"

"Nah..." I plastered myself. My naked cheeks firm upon the cold wall. "I'm good, bro."

He chuckled and rose. The small Jesus piece on his neck glistening. Moving slowly, his dick pointed toward me like an arrow. "Why you so fine, Bambi Kennedy?"

He was now on me. So close I could feel the beat of his heart. Easing down he kissed my neck, the space between my breasts and then my belly. Within seconds his warm tongue flipped my button before easing into my tunnel repeatedly until resisting him was out of the question.

How did he do that?

With my honey on his breath, he rose and kissed my neck again and just like that I was up off my feet as he lifted me in the air. This man was so strong, that he was able to push in and out of me until my body trembled. His lips were against my throat and as he moaned my body vibrated.

He got what he wanted.

Always.

But I would get what I wanted too. To stay in the fucking drug game. I don't care who I had to lay down.

After satisfying Kevin, the rich aroma of freshly brewed coffee greeted me in the kitchen. Wrapped in a red and black robe, I poured myself a cup and stepped out onto the back patio. For a moment, my feet pressed into the cold concrete as I sat in the green lawn chair. The garden was peaceful, which was different from the chaos that filled my mind.

Lately my body had been in pain. The kind of pain that makes no sense since it always happened after making love. I needed to get myself checked but where was the time?

What was happening to me?

Between my body messing with my mental and my son's real estate development deal that was going on in a few weeks, I was overwhelmed. With our backing, my son, Melo, was able to secure a big piece of land in the Baltimore

County area. And he took the money to build what he called Kennedy Court. The property held apartments, upscale restaurants and boutiques. And it was supposed to be our way out of the game.

The brothers were happy. But what about me?

Wanting peace of mind I did what I always do when I want control, hit my yoga mat.

Once in my gym, I roll out my mat and get into downward-facing dog. I don't even hold my position for two breaths before Race rushes inside. "Bambi, We need to talk!"

"Fuck!"

RACE
MOMENTS EARLIER

I love it here and its home, but the Kennedy mansion hides many secrets behind its walls. My lab is one of them.

This is not a run-of-the-mill type spot. It's high-tech and tucked away in a corner of our estate. I do a lot of projects for film companies here, but most of the time I do anything the family needs.

Sitting at my workbench, I'm adjusting the wiring on a mechanical prop when my long black hair gets in the way. Annoyed, I pull the hair band off my wrist and tie it into a tight ponytail. Adjusting my protective goggles to shield my eyes, I suddenly sense a presence behind me. On instinct, I reach for my gun until I realize three things.

First, it's not on my hip because I'm at home. Something I might remedy in the future. And second, no one would be able to get in from the outside if they tried. We saw to that shit because there is no way to get to us from the ground. And third, the violator is my husband.

"What you want, Ramirez?"

I stare him down. Over the years, he looks harder than he has before. Still fine, but more wrinkles covered his face than needed to be there. He was hiding secrets. Some I knew, others I didn't. His soft hair is cut to perfection, and he's wearing a white t and grey sweatpants to try and entice me with that dick print.

Trust me when I say it ain't working.

Before I can react, a pair of lips brush against my neck. I stiffen immediately. I hate being kissed on the neck now, and he knows that shit. We hadn't touched each other in three months. So why start now?

"Get the fuck off me!"

Ramirez doesn't seem fazed. But I know he is. Slowly he shifts slightly, one hand hidden behind his back, and I know he's about to try to get up under my skin again. I don't care what he shows me. I'm gonna keep it together.

"What's behind your back?" I ask calmly. "Since it's obvious you standing over there like a bitch because you want me to know."

"You know how you talk to me is wild. A lesser woman would've been smoked by now."

"I'm a boss first. And you already know what it is. Now what do you want?"

"Where is the sweet girl I once knew?"

"You turned her sour."

"What about now?" He reveals a printout of two tickets to Jamaica.

"I can buy my own getaways. The answer is no."

"Why?"

"Because I don't like you and I don't trust you."

"It's been years since we both agreed to bring Carrie into the relationship."

"I'm not speaking on a dead bitch. You betrayed me when you tried to set off without me. And since then shit ain't been no better. I'm good with it. Are you?"

"We betrayed each other, but that's how shit be when you do what we do." He walks up to me and says, "Race, I fucked up. But in our life, we deal in coke, loyalty and betrayal. You take out one and we not the Kennedys no more."

"Hold up, so you justifying cheating on me?"

"We both fucked that bitch! And didn't you have to betray someone you loved before? I mean you betrayed everybody when you slept with Bradley."

I look at my door. "Keep your voice down!" I thought about how I had Scarlett jumped all those years back because she was with him. But I was no better because I used Bradley to get at Ramirez. "I never did nothing."

"You a fucking lie! And what I'm saying is that for us, shit like that happens sometimes. When it did with us, with me fucking Scarlett and getting closer to Carrie, I was in my villain era. You were too. But all I want to do now is love on my woman. Love on my wife."

"Well you betta go find one quick. Now what you want, Ramirez? Outside of your weak ass offer to fly me some place else."

He sighed and dragged a long hand down his face. "I got a few things I want to talk about. We need to discuss our marriage. Which is why I bought the vacation."

I turn back to my work. "I'm busy. So like I been screaming, if you came to discuss our relationship, get the fuck up out of here. I ain't dealing with niggas who cheat."

I don't know what he's doing because my eyes are now on the device I'm building, but I can feel his heat. "It's about that shipment to Garrison Projects."

I shake my head. "You mean the one they stole from your people? On your fucking watch."

He shuffles. Embarrassed probably. "Yeah, that one."

He sighs.

"It mysteriously showed back up."

I look up from my work. "Showed back up? How…how did that happen?"

He hesitates. "I don't know. But I got a call that the bricks were back."

"Everything in place?"

"Yep, I distributed it to my crew and everything. Since my people got held up after it was gone I figured it was time to make some money again."

I remove my goggles and set them down, my mind racing. "Ram, this doesn't seem right. I mean who made the call to resupply your people without a convo?"

"I did."

"This isn't just random acts of kindness." I stand up. "I need to find Bambi. We need to figure out what's going on."

Without another word, I turn to leave the lab, but he grabs me. Looking down at me, I can see how our failed marriage is tearing him apart. It's doing the same for me but in a different way.

"Can you honestly say you don't want me no more? I mean, what would you do without me?"

I don't answer and instead, I pull away.

The tension between us remains unresolved because I don't trust him. Ever since we brought another woman into our marriage and I discovered that he had fallen in love, and ever since he slept with Scarlett, his deceased brother's wife and my ex-friend, we couldn't breathe naturally in front of one another.

And I miss him.

I do.

But more than anything I miss the memory of what we had!

As I hurry through the mansion's halls, my mind is focused on the new threat. And there was only one person in the world I trusted enough to talk about it with.

Bambi Kennedy.

DENIM

This morning, I'm sitting at the breakfast table, trying to focus on the article in front of me on my phone. There had been a string of men who had been victimized in the streets of D.C. by a strange woman. Each held stories from theft to physical harm, but all were consistent in one right: the woman gave them the creeps, but they gave her time anyway.

Just like niggas to want to fuck a dark hole.

As I'm reading the article, Maureen, our chef, and her team place plates laden with breakfast delicacies in front of us, pausing my read. The aroma of freshly cooked food fills the air, but I don't have much of an appetite.

Just as I place my phone down, wearing a black silk robe and a curly temple taper, Bradley, my husband, sits across from me, his attention divided between his phone and the plate of eggs and bacon in front of him. The gold chain on his bare chest shines with light movement. He glances up occasionally, and I smile, but as usual, he seems mostly distracted or uninterested.

Kevin joins us a few minutes later, wearing no t-shirt and red sweatpants. He looks equally preoccupied with his phone. Ramirez enters next.

Then, in a rush of wind, Master, Scarlett's nine-year-old son, sits next to me. He's such a cutie pie and immediately begins to grab my face with his wet hands while plastering boy kisses all over my cheeks. He does this every single morning, making me his biggest fan.

I pour all of my love and attention onto Master, like I gave birth to him myself. He's biracial, a mixture of his mother's pale skin and his father's chocolate tone. Scarlett, his estranged mother, left him in our care years ago. Because of it, he calls all the ladies in the Kennedy family "Mom," but I'm the only one he refers to as "Mommy." Somewhere down deep though, I know he longs for his mother's love.

That's where we were different.

My mother, Sarah, was out there somewhere but I didn't care. She betrayed me too many times. I put her up in the most luxurious homes, gave her money and she still chose my sister Grainger, who was murdered for her deeds against my family, over me. My last act of love for that bitch was when I cut my dreads. The next act of love for myself was when I grew them back. So outside of the Kennedy's I don't have no family.

I giggle before buttering Master's toast. "When you wash your hands, you gotta dry them too."

"You should let him do that shit himself," Bradley says to me pointing to the bread. "You a big man, right, nephew?"

Oh, so he does see me.

"I am, but if a woman wants to butter my bread, why not let her?"

Ramirez laughs. "Hold up, what you know about what a woman wants?"

"Yeah, where you learn all that grown nigga talk?" Bradley asks.

"Nowhere. I'm smart that way. Y'all need to take lessons on how to treat a woman." He turns to Ramirez. "Can I play in your man cave later? With my paint gun?"

"That's a wild ass transition," Bradley says. "He goes from talking about women and then asks if he can play in a nigga's man cave."

"No and don't go in there, man," Ramirez tells him. "I told you that before."

I frown. "What you do in there anyway?"

He grabs a piece of bacon and pops it in his mouth, ignoring the fuck out of me.

"Aye, Denim, where's Race and Bambi?" Kevin asks, his tone breaking the mood.

You know what, in the dead of night, I hear Bambi calling his name in the bedroom as she gets her back banged out, but with me, he was always in business mode. He was the direct connect to our Mexican drug supplier Suarez Vidal, and I believe the pressure of always having to look over his shoulder was starting to get to him. Especially after all these years, Suarez's main US connect was Mitch, who Bambi murdered, causing Kevin fear. In other words he was always concerned that Suarez would come for his head, which made him want to get out.

"Denim, where is Race and Bambi?"

When Kevin asks me the question again, Bradley looks at me, raising an eyebrow. I take a deep breath, trying to keep my voice steady. "I don't know. They don't tell me anything anymore."

There's a bitterness in my words that I can't hide. It's a sore spot, this lack of trust from my sisters. I used to be in the loop, part of their inner circle. Now, I'm left on the outside, a spectator in my own family.

"Mommy, are you okay?"

See what I'm saying? The boy loves me, and the feeling is mutual. Master's presence has been a calm for my wounded heart. My daughter was killed in a fire, and since then, I've welcomed his attention and affection. He's a sweet, sensitive boy, and taking care of him gives my life purpose. Which is odd because I couldn't stand his fucking mother who I haven't seen in over eight years.

And I was fine with it to be honest. Because I'll never forget the time she watched my daughter when she was alive, which ended up with her being in the hospital.

Suddenly, Bambi and Race enter. They don't even bother to sit at the table. Instead, they remain standing on some professional shit. I figured it was about the Kennedy Court unveiling that Melo was heading up but the expression on their faces told me I was wrong.

"We have a situation that's not making much sense," Bambi announces as everyone, even Master, listens.

"What's going on?" Kevin asks.

"I believe we're under attack. But I don't know by who."

"Attack is a bit much. They gave the product back," Ramirez says.

Kevin frowns. "Hold up, the weight came back?"

Ramirez nods.

"Why you ain't tell us?" He yells.

"Because I told Race!"

"This nigga using family business information as bait to get back with his wife," Bradley laughs. "News flash, nigga. She still don't wanna fuck with you!"

"Fuck you just say?" Ramirez yells.

"Stop all this extra shit!" Bambi steps closer to the table, bumping it slightly. "Listen, the fact that they gave the product back is an issue because it means someone is playing a mental game. We may need to call off the Kennedy Court—."

"No, we not either!" Kevin says. "That unveiling is the entry way to our new life. So there's no need to do anything right now. Let's just play shit by ear."

CHAPTER TWO
SCARLETT

I sit behind my sleek, modern desk. Its morning, but the shades are drawn the way I prefer. There's a mirror, and when I look into it, despite the low light in my office casting a weird glow on the walls, they still highlight my raised red scars from the past. Both physical and emotional, these wounds have left me with memories of the people I will always hate.

In the corner of my office, Zayden, my seven-year-old son, plays quietly with his toys. For a moment his innocent laughter breaks the dark thoughts that cloud my mind and makes me angrier. Because I have another child out in the world. One who should be with me, but instead he is with the Kennedy's and will never get to know me.

His own fucking mother!

"Still working?" My boyfriend asks.

Johnathan enters deeper into my space. His chocolate skin glows lightly when he steps closer, and I wish I could appreciate the fact that he was mine. A skydiver for a living, as adventurous as he is I'm always surprised at how he tries so hard to soothe my boring soul.

Because After all these years, I can't forget how Race Kennedy ordered me jumped. Changing the course of my life forever.

9 YEARS EARLIER

Banished from the Kennedy's and the Kennedy king mansion, Scarlett sat on the park bench biting her nails while waiting on Race. When she saw Race walking in the park pushing a designer black buggy with Scarlett's son Master inside she held her trembling lips as they approached. She never realized how much she missed both of them until that moment.

Standing in front of Race she said, "Can I hug you?"

Race sighed and extended her palm. "Not yet, Scarlett. Not yet."

"I respect that and understand." She looked down at Master. "Can I...pick him up?"

"Of course...He's your baby and he needs you."

Slowly Scarlett lowered her body and raised up her child. "I can tell he's being loved. Thank you for this...so much."

"We gonna look after him, Scarlett. You know that. Blood born Kennedy's are the only ones safe for true love."

"Thank you."

"Why, Scarlett?" Race asked. "Why did you do it?" Scarlett placed Master in the carriage and sat down on the wooden bench. She was speaking on how she fucked Ramirez behind her back.

Race flopped next to her and waited for the answer.

"Loneliness has a way of temporarily blinding you, Race. Making you feel like any attention you get in the moment is all that matters. Not making excuses but you can't see the consequences for your actions, nor do you want to. It's like a drug and I was wrong."

They spoke a bit longer and then Scarlett said, "All I want to do is come home. Can I? Please."

"Take this for now." Race dug into her purse and handed her ten thousand dollars. "I'm definitely gonna talk to the fam. But I need to know if you do come back that I can trust you."

"You can trust me, Race. And I'm done with Ramirez. Sisters before misters."

Race laughed. "Corny but I like it." She ran her hand down the side of Scarlett's beautiful face. "But first..." Race rose up.

"First what?"

"I have to make a few alterations."

Scarlett giggled. "What you talking about, Race?"

"Like I said, I have to change some things up before letting you back in the home."

Scarlett was so focused on Race's expression that she didn't see the five women from the hood she hired walking behind her. Their expressions showed they meant business. "Race....don't do this...I'm begging you."

"Beat her ass!" Race ordered. "Paying special attention to that face. I want it real fucked up."

Pushing the carriage with one hand, Race walked away, Scarlett's screams behind her.

Scarlett never returned to the mansion.

The beatdown was so severe that it cracked the top of her skull resulting in a gash that extended from her scalp right onto her forehead. To the day, due to awkward positioning, not even a wig could hide it. Next since she could not breathe on her own, a trachea had to be placed in her throat, and so when it was removed, unfortunately it left a permanent mark at the base of her neck.

When she woke up outside of pain the only thing she felt was hate. Hate for the Kennedy sisters and hate for herself for being so gullible. For wanting love. For needing love.

When she was well, using some of the ten thousand dollars Race gave her she rented a room from a motel. Eating only bread for breakfast, lunch and dinner she eventually got a job in the same motel as a maid. Time after time men would try to fuck her for money but she decided she would no longer let someone use her body for pleasure. Instead she starved and saved every dime she had until she was able to get enough to rent an apartment. After that, she continued to clean rooms, but requested more hours because her goal was clear.

She never wanted to be at the mercy of another bitch, ho or nigga again.

Her life was balancing out and then she saw her son on television with the Kennedys. They were talking about the groundwork being laid for a new development, and her son was there, holding onto Denim like he was her own.

Devastated, a new plan developed in her mind.

She went to a skydiving center. Her instructor, Johnathan, explained the process and took her up in a flight. But when he caught her rushing toward the open door without a harness, ready to end her life, he held onto her with all his strength. Alone in the back, it took everything in him to pin her down. He couldn't even close the door.

"I don't know what has happened to you, but this is not it!" He yelled to be heard over the roaring wind.

"You don't understand! I have nothing! I have no one!"

"Use that anger! Use that rage! Don't take your own life. Take theirs instead!"

Three things happened after that. Firstly, she decided not to take her own life. Secondly, he became her man, eventually showing her how to skydive to relieve stress. And thirdly, she mastered cryptocurrency. With her quiet demeanor and unwavering focus, she excelled, even though money would not come overnight.

It was at that time that she met Ovay, a low-level drug dealer when she opened his door to clean his room. "I'm sorry," she said backing out. "I'll come back later."

Ovay had scars all over his face, from popped acne bumps that left their mark on his cocoa skin. "You ain't got to clean my room." He wiped his hand on his crisp white t-shirt and rose. "Just give me some fresh sheets."

With the door slightly cracked she said, "Are you sure?"

He nodded. "Unless you want to wipe off cum stains and used condoms."

Removing the sheets off her cart, she handed them to him. He brushed her finger with his and she pulled back quickly. When she turned to walk away, he begin to laugh.

She frowned and turned around. "What's funny?"

"You ugly. And I ain't never seen no ugly redhead in my life." He gripped his dick. "Y'all strawberry head bitches usually be cute as fuck."

She looked down. Defeated by an even uglier man. She already knew what her face was giving, the last thing she needed was him telling her. So, she hit it for the door again.

"Listen, the way your face looks you better get used to being called ugly. Ain't no need in being soft. If I were you I'd give myself a nickname so – ."

"But you ain't me!"

"Scarlett..."

Her eyes widened and she looked at him harshly. "You know me?"

"What happened to you? You used to be hard. At least when you were with them."

"How do you know my name?"

"Scarlett Kennedy." He scratched his scalp. "One fourth part of the Pretty Kings. Of course I know you. You a living legend. And I know what them bitches did to you too. Had you whipped and then got the nerve to throw themselves into real estate. While you cleaning one of the buildings they own."

She glared. "What you talking about?"

"They own this raggedy ass bitch!" He laughed. "At least their son Melo does." He shook his head. "The thing is the nigga don't even live here. He live out Houston. So you cleaning this bitch is some serendipitous shit ain't it?"

Scarlett was livid. The fact that she was cleaning a Kennedy king building let her know at the very least today would be her last day. You not here by accident, are you? You...you came for me?"

Silence.

She planted her feet and raised her head high. "Did they send you? To finish me off."

"Nah...I legit came here to find you. You have some specific information I need."

"Me?"

"Yes. You ready to get back to work, and be the pretty king you really are?"

"Scarlett, did you hear me?" Johnathan asked. He towered over me and placed his hand on the small of my back.

"Yeah...um...I did." I ruffled my son's hair.

"So are you still working on something?" He pulls me closer, and I can feel his thickness on my belly because he's taller than me. He's dry begging for some pussy. I wish he'd just ask and get it over with.

My phone buzzes on the desk, breaking his questioning. I glance at the screen and see a message from my best friend. I wiggle away and pick up the phone. My eyes narrow as I read the details. My boyfriend sees it too. I didn't feel him staring over my shoulder.

"Scarlett, you still on that revenge shit? After all this time."

"Why are you in my business?"

"I asked you a fucking question." He's angry but I can hear the underlying concern. He knows my obsession consumes me.

I shake my head, unable to tear my eyes away from the screen. "I can't. I tried to let it go. I really did. But I won't be better until—"

"Until what? Huh? What about our family? What about what we're building?"

He places a hand on my shoulder, trying to offer comfort. "You're better than this shit. Don't let them bitches drag you back down because you want what you agreed to let go."

I look up at him. "Do you remember what you said the first day you met me?"

"What are you—."

"Do you remember?"

"I said a lot of things."

"You said, *"Use that anger! Use that rage! Don't take your own life. Take theirs instead!"* I pause. "So if I don't get what's mine, then that's exactly what the fuck I will do."

CHAPTER THREE
BAMBI

B reakfast is a tense affair.

As we sit around the table, the aroma of freshly cooked food fills the air, but there's a whiff of tension. Kevin, Bradley, Ramirez, Race, Denim, and Master are all still here, but my mind is already racing with possibilities when I hear it—a soft whirring noise outside. I ignore it, believing it's another airplane moving not too far away from our home.

I move a little in my seat. "I know we going in circles but like I said, them stealing our package is not about money. They want us to know we've wronged them in other ways."

Denim looks confused. "How? What do you mean?"

Race steps in, her voice low but firm. "If we knew that, we would handle the situation and be done with it."

I shake my head. "I want all of you to talk to your men." I look at Kevin and his brothers. "See if they have seen anything, like who brought the package back. Car. Looks. Height. I don't care what it is tell us everything, no matter how small."

"I've already spoken to Suarez," Kevin said. "And told him to hold off before sending anything else. Because the pack being returned or not, I don't trust it either."

I stare at him. "You gave that order before speaking to us?" I say. "You know how they get when they can't move product and other sets can."

"Yeah. I wanted to—."

"No moves without a vote, Kevin. That was your rule not mine."

"Well, I pushed off anyway."

I try to remain calm, but my rage is all in my eyes.

Suddenly, the soft whirring noise outside grows louder. This is not a plane. It's something else. We all freeze, our ears straining to catch the sound. It's unmistakable now, a constant, mechanical hum.

"What the fuck is that?" Kevin asks, his voice tight with concern.

I rush to the window, my heart pounding. My breath catches in my chest as I see the morning sky filled with hundreds of black drones. There are so many that it looks like a flock of crows has descended upon us.

"Denim, take Master to his room." My gaze remains outside. "Now!"

I turn to her, and she hesitates.

"What the fuck you waiting on? Move!"

"But I don't wanna go. I want to help!"

"We don't need your help," Bradley says. "We need you to protect the boy."

Finally, she grabs Master, who starts to protest, but she shoves him out of the dining room anyway. Once they're gone, we move quickly and efficiently, each of us retrieving our weapons from hidden compartments around the house. Under floorboards. In secret closets. Even with being fully loaded and ready, we still had enough artillery hidden to start and end a war.

My heart pounds in my chest as I strap on my gear. This isn't just about protecting ourselves. It's about protecting our home and everything we've built. Why did it seem like every few years or so, somebody was always trying us? I was born for war. But I knew that with Kevin wanting to get out, this would be all the excuse he needed.

We group at the front door, weapons in hand. The soft whirring of the drones is louder now, almost deafening. How many are out there? Glancing to my right, Kevin is at my side. To my left is Race. Bradley and Ramirez take up the rear. "Y'all ready?" I say.

My husband nods. "Take them down!" Kevin shouts.

We step out onto the front lawn, and the sight of the drones swarming above us is both surreal and terrifying. Immediately we spread out, taking aim at the sky. The air is filled with the sound of gunfire as we unleash hundreds of bullets. Shells fall to the earth. My focus narrows. Each shot is calculated, deliberate. I take a deep breath and fire more, hitting one drone after another as I watch them fall.

My family does their best, but I'm in the zone so they're not as accurate as me. After all the military prepared me for moments like this. One after another, they continue to drop, crashing onto the lawn and driveway like dead flies.

And then, suddenly, some of the drones rush away, and before long, things are peaceful again. Only the sounds of our breathing remain, telling me what we already know. Somebody wants to fuck with our minds.

As quickly as it began, it ends. With no one hurt.

I lower my weapon, breathing heavily. Around me, the lawn is littered with the broken remains of the drones.

Kevin winks. "You did good."

It sounds patronizing but go off. I nod in response.

"Let's see if we can find out what these are about," Ramirez says as we all spread out.

"I'm gonna grab a box to look at these bitches later in my lab." She runs off.

Broken fragment after fragment, we pick up pieces. As my hand moves over the hard plastics, I have no more information about who is responsible. Suddenly, I see something at the far end of the field that makes me squint. It's colorful...light blue and appears...well...like a stuffed animal.

I reload my rifle and aim at it. When I get close, I see exactly what it is. So I shoot it, opening its insides, causing it to bleed cotton.

"Is that a bunny?" Kevin questions, moving past me to pick it up from the ground.

I didn't see him there.

Had I seen it first, I would have blown it deeper into the soil. Because the only bunny I knew was his aunt. Whom he loved. And whom I murdered.

I walk into our bedroom, my heart still pounding from the adrenaline of the drone attack. As I enter, I freeze at the doorway, my eyes locking onto Kevin. He's standing there, holding the bullet riddled soiled stuffed bunny we found outside like it's a little dead homie.

Why is he doing this?

The sight of it in his hands sends a shiver down my spine. To me, it represents too many secrets. Secrets of the past which eventually were revealed. Leaving me consumed with jealousy and rage. Even in death, that evil woman, his aunt, haunts my days.

Why shouldn't I be angry? He slept with a blood family member. Granted it started when he was young, but when he was old enough to know better, I believe it continued, with her even wanting to replace me and take up position.

"Did you look through that thing? To make sure it doesn't have a camera?"

"I'm not stupid. I went in through the hole you left into it. It's clean."

"Are you sure?"

Kevin looks up, his eyes filled with pain. "I miss her, Bambi. Even after all this time, I still miss my aunt."

Fuck he telling me for?

I hesitate, unsure of how to respond. The guilt of knowing I killed her misses my heart, so I have no fucks to give. At all. We needed to meet with the Russians when we thought Kevin was dead, and she had stolen the number necessary to make the call. So I met her at her house, and when she didn't give me the paper she stole from my safe, I took her life instead.

Of course it was many, many years ago. But the feelings were still raw. "I know, Kevin. I miss her too."

He shakes his head, his grip tightening on the bunny. "So you lie to me now?"

Oh shit!

I had gone too far. Everyone knew I couldn't stand that big bitch in life or death.

"I'm sorry. I just...I know what she meant to you. Or what she means to you."

"I feel like less of a man because although I love you, had I not been gone, causing you to kill her, she would be alive."

Why? So you could bump coochies?

I shiver. "Kevin, Bunny was your aunt, but she was a snake. You know that right?" I step closer.

"None of us are perfect! Especially not you."

My pulse quickens, and I can't help the defensive edge that creeps into my voice. "Where does your loyalty lie, Kevin? With your family here, now, or with your dead aunt? I mean we had drones hanging over our house and the only thing you can think about is a fucking bunny?"

"My dead aunt?" His eyes flash with hurt and betrayal. "How can you even say it like that? She was family too. So of course family matters."

I swallow hard, my hands trembling. "I'm asking because we have to stay focused on the present. On the threats we face now. Again have you forgotten about the fucking drones over our home?"

Before Kevin can respond, Denim appears in the doorway. She's annoyed. I've known her long enough to tell before she opens her mouth. "We need to talk," she demands, cutting through the tension.

I glance between Kevin and Denim, my mind racing. The conversation with Kevin isn't over, I can tell.

His jaw tightens, and he's still clutching the stuffed bunny with all his sensitive heart. I can even see its head bend backward. "I gotta go."

"This isn't over, Bambi."

"I didn't think it was." I move to grab the toy. "Let me throw this away." I reach for it, but he uses his free hand to shove me in the middle of the chest. Right where he kissed some hours earlier.

"Don't play with me. Now is not the time!" He storms away, bunny in hand like a bitch.

On my son's dick, this nigga gonna make me snap.

CHAPTER FOUR
DENIM

I stand in the living room, my arms crossed, trying to keep my composure. Bambi is propped in front of me, her face etched with irritation, while Race sits back on the couch, her eyes glued to her phone, scrolling through her texts as if what I'm about to say doesn't matter. I can tell Bambi's mood is off, likely because of some conversation she had with Kevin before I entered.

But for real, I don't care. I've had enough of being pushed aside.

"You know what? I'm tired of this," I say, my voice cutting through the room like a knife. Both of them look up. "I'm tired of being taken advantage of. I'm tired of y'all acting like I'm not even in the room!"

Bambi's eyes narrow. "Denim, where is all this coming from?"

"You know exactly what I'm talking about. Every time there's a problem, y'all handle it without me. Every time a decision needs to be made, y'all make it without even asking what I think."

Race finally looks up from her phone, her expression dismissive. "Girl, you do a great job of picking the wrong time to call a fucking meeting. I want to look through those drone pieces to see if I can find out who is behind it. So get to your point or I'm out."

"Really, Race? That's all you've got to say. I'm standing here, pouring my heart out, and you can't even bother to listen."

Bambi moves closer, her eyes cold. "You want to talk so let's go. Maybe if you stepped the fuck up a bit more, we wouldn't have to make all the decisions without you. Maybe if you were thorough enough, we could trust you. But we both know you not. Because you don't make a fucking move unless Bradley gives the okay."

Her words sting, and I feel a surge of anger. "I respect my husband. And me asking his input—."

"How often does Bradley ask you for input before he makes a move?" Race says. "He tells you how it's done, and you roll with it."

"That's not true!"

Race shakes her head, her tone condescending. "Denim, what about the job we gave you in D.C.? All you had to do was make sure Rafeel wasn't stepping on our shit and claiming it was Kennedy coke on the street. What you do?

Go talk to Bradley about it and then tell us you couldn't do it."

"Faked a headache and everything," Bambi says.

"And when I came to you about it you start crying and begging for a shoulder to lean on."

"You see what I'm saying," Bambi adds. "We can't count on you. If we can't count on you, we can't trust you," she moves closer. "You're a mother again. A real good mother at that. Stay there. Leave the gangster shit to us."

The room falls silent, the tension thick. My hands tremble, and I take a deep breath, trying to steady myself.

"That was a low blow," I say, my body trembling. "I lost a baby just like you lost a child. Now I don't know what the fuck you and Kevin going through, but don't take it out on me, bitch."

"Fuck you just call me?" She steps to me.

"Not now," Race says rushing between us.

It's then that I notice Bradley, dipping toward the door with a large navy-blue duffle bag slung over his shoulder. An overnight bag at that.

"Bradley!" I call out, my voice cracking. "Where you going?"

"You see what I'm saying? You don't even know what he up to half the time." She pauses. "You done with us?" Race asks. "Because we got shit to do."

"For now." I rush behind him just as he moves toward the door. "Bradley, what's going on?"

He freezes, his back to me. The silence is deafening.

"You leaving?" I ask, my heart pounding. "Right now, in the middle of a war!"

Bradley turns slowly. "I wanna follow a lead I believe is connected to all this shit. So I gotta go check it out."

I can feel the tears welling up, but I blink them back, refusing to let them fall. This only proves Bambi's point that he never asks my opinion on shit. "And you think leaving without telling me is the answer?"

He doesn't respond, just stands there.

"Fine," I say, my voice barely above a whisper. "Go. But don't expect everything to be the same when you get back."

Bradley nods, not saying another word. He turns and walks out the door, the sound of it closing behind him echoing through the room. I take a deep breath, turning back to Bambi and Race leaving the living room.

I need a friend right now. Instead, I watch them both walk away, my heart aching with the weight of their words and Bradley's dismissal. For the first time, I realize just how alone I am.

So I go to the one place that makes me feel good.

To see about Master.

CHAPTER FIVE
SCARLETT

I'm cruising through the city in my white G-Wagon, the low hum of the engine barely audible over the heavy bass blasting through the speakers. I like it that way so I can't hear my own thoughts.

I feel off balance, but I look cute even though I don't know why. My outfit, a crimson jumpsuit with long sleeves and a low neckline, clings to my body. The material stretches down to my feet and meets my white sneakers. I feel powerful, untouchable, ready for whatever the night throws my way.

As I navigate through the city, my mind races as I take a sharp turn into a narrow, dimly lit alley. The darkness envelopes my white truck as I slow down, scanning the shadows for my contact.

Within moments, Bradley steps out from the darkness, his expression tense and heated. I pull the truck to a stop and ease out, the cool night air hitting my skin, but I barely feel it. My focus is entirely on the man in front of me.

"Scarlett," he greets me with a nod. "I see you still as ugly inside as you are out."

"What did you just say to me?" I reply, confused at how he's coming at me. We normally don't move like this towards each other.

"You heard me loud and clear."

"Bradley, what is this about?"

"Are you responsible for what happened today at my fucking house?"

I tilt my head. "I don't know what you mean."

His eyes flash with anger. "Don't play games with me, bitch! The drones, Scarlett! Did you have anything to do with drones over my crib?"

"What exactly did the drones do?"

He steps closer, his presence intimidating, but I stand my ground.

"I've agreed to meet you yearly so you can receive updates on your son. But if I find out this was your doing, I will unleash hell on your fucking life like you can't imagine, bitch. Do you understand?"

I narrow my eyes. After all, who does he think he's talking to? The dumb little white girl back in the day who let everyone walk all over her. I may retain the Kennedy name, but I am anything but their step wife anymore.

"Let me be clear, you ain't doing me any favors. That boy is of my blood! And I deserve to know what's going on with him."

"He's my brother's blood too! And mine!"

"That nigga dead! He's my fucking blood in the here and now!" I yell louder, pointing at the ground. "And nothing will keep me from getting updates on him. Nothing. You better remember that before you threaten me again."

Bradley's jaw clenches. "Don't push me, Scarlett."

"You don't push me! You have no idea about the storms I'm capable of," I step closer. "You think you can intimidate me? Think again. I've been through hell and I'm not afraid to take you with me."

His glare intensifies. "Consider this your last warning."

I watch him turn and walk back into the shadows before slowly disappearing from sight.

Sliding back into my G-Wagon, I grip the steering wheel tightly, my knuckles whiter with rage. The game is far from over, and Bradley's threats only fuel my hate for that family.

The anger still boils over as Bradley's threats echo in my mind. I crank up the volume on my radio, Nicki Minaj's voice yelling at me through the car's speakers to be harder. The way he spoke to me reminds me so much of how they spoke to me back in the day.

I'm different. I'm different. I'm different. I repeat this over like an affirmation to stop the noise. But it's not working. As I drive away from the alley, the streetlights reflecting off my car, I grab my phone and dial my best friend Electra. She was smart like me but more than anything, she was loyal. With her I was an equal. Not the token white girl they could rage out on when the streets got them down.

"Tell me again why I have the world in front of me and I should let it go," I demand as soon as she picks up. My voice is tight, my knuckles white on the steering wheel. "Tell me how I'm not who I used to be."

Electra's voice is bright and giggly. "Okay, it's playtime." She clears her throat. "Scarlett, you're smart, you're the boss, you're a millionaire, and everyone loves you. You've got it all, girl! A man who adores you and a son who worships the ground you walk on. What's better than that?"

I swallow hard, the weight of everything pressing down on me. "And tell me again why I should let my son stay with the Kennedy's?"

Silence.

"Scarlett, I...because...um..." Electra fumbles, unable to find the words. "I mean we have a plan. It's working. Maybe you should —."

"Forget it," I snap, hanging up the phone. My grip tightens on the steering wheel, and I slam my foot on the gas.

The night air is cool as it rushes in through the open window. I had to speed, but eventually I spot Bradley's Rolls Royce ahead before he merges on the highway. It's sleek and black against the dimly lit street. Without a second thought, I veer towards it, my G-Wagon smashing into the side of his car. The impact sends his vehicle spinning.

When it stops, I jump out, adrenaline pumping through my veins. The sound of crunching metal fills the air as I yank open Bradley's door. He's holding his head, disoriented.

"What's wrong with you?! Are you crazy?"

"You forgot to let me see my son," I say, my voice low and dangerous.

Bradley looks up, confusion and pain etched on his face. "What? I don't get it."

"You lured me here by saying you would update me on Master," I say, my patience thin. "And that's why I came. You didn't show me any videos or give me pictures and that makes you a fucking liar." My breath is heavy.

He doesn't answer, must be too dizzy from the crash. I reach into his car and grab his phone.

"Get out of —"

He tries to protest, but I snatch the bitch anyway. Within seconds, I'm already back in my G-Wagon, peeling out of there before he can stop me.

As I speed away, I glance in the rearview mirror. Bradley is still slumped in his seat. But I notice something...someone hiding in the shadows I hadn't seen before.

Who was that?

CHAPTER SIX
DENIM

I grip the steering wheel, my knuckles turning white as I try to keep my emotions in check. The city lights blur past me as I follow Bradley's broken car at a distance. I can't believe this shit! I literally saw him go meet another woman!

Another woman.

Who the fuck was she?!

My heart aches, and I don't understand why this is happening. Bradley had always been there for me. He had always been mine. Why the fuck has that changed?

I'm a good wife!

A good fucking wife!

As mad as I was, I was relieved he was okay after she hit his car. I almost ran to him, but anger took over, so I let him figure shit out on his own. And after witnessing the accident from the woman I couldn't make out; I watch him close his broke car door and drive away.

I dial his number, my fingers trembling. It seems like forever, but he picks up after a few rings.

"Hey, baby," he says, his voice uneven but I know why. He was just in an accident. "Now is not a good time."

I swallow the lump in my throat. I feel like I can't talk but I must say something. "Where are you?" I ask, trying to keep my voice steady.

"What you talking about? I'm out of town, handling business. I told you that already."

My blood boils at his lie. I can see him up ahead because I'm following. Close enough to see his every move but not close enough for him to see mine. "You sure about that?"

"Yeah, why you keep asking?"

I watch as he pulls into the driveway of a gas station. "I see you right now, my nigga. I saw the accident too."

There's a pause on the other end. He's been caught. "What…what you talking about?"

I take a deep breath, trying to keep my composure. "I'm talking about you fucking lying to me, Bradley!"

I can tell he tries to sound calm, but I can hear the panic in his voice. "Denim, you tripping, baby. Look, let me turn back and come home. So we can talk."

"But I thought you were out of town." He doesn't know about the Air Tag I put in his car months ago. But I do. I never had a reason to check for his location until now. I'm so glad he uses a Droid and didn't get notified of its presence.

"I am out of town but—"

"You're a liar. And a bad one at that." I speed up and pull into the gas station, parking in front of him. Still on the phone I say, "So my question to you is this, you still wanna lie or finally tell the truth?"

His headlights are blasting right into my face, mine are doing the same to him. When I squint, I can see his eyes widen, I guess realizing he's been caught. I also notice his forehead is bleeding a little.

Why don't I care?

He steps out in front of my car. "Denim, it's not what it looks like," the phone dangles in his grasp.

I get out, my anger boiling over. "Save it," I say, my voice shaking with rage. "But what I do want to know is this. Who the fuck was that white bitch? Huh?"

He squints. "Wait...you didn't...you—."

"Who was she?!"

Silence.

"When did we get here, Bradley? We've always been better than this."

For a moment nothing else is said. Instead, we stand in the dimly lit gas station lot, the tension between us thick. After all it should be. I caught my husband in a lie. He steps closer, reaching out to me. "Denim, I'm sorry. I didn't want to hurt you. Let me explain what's—"

"You didn't want to hurt me?" I laugh bitterly. "You've been hurting me for a long time. Why apologize now? You said you were out of town, and you lied. So I don't need your excuses. I'm done."

I turn on my heels and get back into my car, slamming the door shut. I can hear him calling my name, but I don't look back right away. When I finally do, he's on the phone, probably calling her again.

I speed off faster, my mind scattered, my vision blurred and my heart in shambles.

CHAPTER SEVEN
BAMBI

I sit in my office, the door closed against the noise of the Kennedy Kings talking in the house. Before me, spread out on the wide desk, is a large sheet of paper covered with names and places, each one meticulously noted. It's a web of connections, detailing everyone with a grudge against me, my family, and our empire. I put everyone I could think of on the list, but no one makes sense. Half of these grievances had been resolved in death or money.

So who wanted smoke now?

The drone attack has me on fucking edge, and I'm determined to find out who's behind it and what they might do next.

I hear quick footsteps and my eyes flicker to the doorway as I see Denim dip past. She sounds as if she's been crying. She's always fucking crying, and I can only imagine what happened now.

Where is Race? I need her!

I shove my chair back, the legs scraping against the floor, and march out of my office. I find Kevin, the nigga I'm looking for in the moment in the living room. All posted up talking to Ramirez like a bitch.

Without waiting for a pause in their conversation, I cut in, "I'm going to question Ramirez's people. After that package was stolen and mysteriously returned, I believe it was related to the drone attack. Unless y'all know something I don't."

"Don't do that," Ramirez begs. "I done already spoke to them!"

"Why you protecting them so much?"

Kevin's head snaps towards me, his eyes narrowing. "Bambi, you need to stand down."

I cross my arms over my chest. "I can't do that, Kevin. I won't."

He steps closer, his voice low and commanding. "I'm telling you to stand the fuck down! As my wife and as my employee."

I hold his gaze. "Y'all better do something and quick. Or me and Race moving in."

Without waiting for his response, I turn on my heels and head back to my office, slamming the door behind me.

Once alone I grab my phone and dial Race's number. It rings, and each second feels like an eternity. "Race, where the fuck are you?" I ask as soon as she picks up.

RACE

MOMENTS EARLIER

The cigar lounge is dimly lit, with a thick haze of smoke swirling around, casting a shadowy ambiance over the room. The air is rich with the scent of burning tobacco, a heady mixture of earthy, spicy, and woody notes in the air. The low hum of conversation meshes with the occasional clinking of glasses and I'm at peace.

I come here a lot.

Each time as a different person.

I sit at a small table meant for two, dressed in one of my many disguises. Today, I'm wearing a dark auburn wig, facial prosthetics that alter the shape of my nose and cheekbones, and large red glasses that obscure my eyes. To set my trap, my titties are shined up and look edible. Presenting just what my prey needs to come my way. The persona is complete with a tailored suit that fits my body snugly, making me look every bit the mysterious businesswoman hiding in plain sight. No one would recognize me as Race Kennedy, and that's precisely the point.

As I take a slow drag from my cigar, savoring the way the smoke fills my cheeks before exhaling it in a controlled puff, I notice another man approaching. This is the third one today. I grab my phone, snap his picture without him seeing and look at the info on my screen.

He sits down across from me, his eyes lingering on my body instead of my face. "Mind if I join you?" He asks, his voice smooth.

I sit my phone face down, blow another puff of smoke, letting it drift lazily between us. "Not at all," I reply, my voice altered slightly by the prosthetics.

As he settles in, my eyes are drawn to the light ring band area on his finger. If I was a gambler, I would say the jewelry that would let a person know he's married is in his pocket. It's a familiar sight, that pisses me off. Why marry if you want to be a whore and take off your ring? I guess I could say the same thing to myself.

He leans in, trying to make small talk, but I'm barely listening. Instead, I focus on the way his ringless hand catches the dim light, a whisper of a promise he's breaking. After a few minutes of his mumbling, he shifts in his seat.

"What you want with me?" I ask straight up. "You've been talking a lot and not saying shit."

He laughs. "Straight to the point huh?"

Silence.

"How about we get out of here? Go for a ride."

This is exactly what I was waiting for. "Sure," I say, my voice calm and controlled. "Lead the way."

He stands up, offering his hand, and I take it, allowing him to pull me out of the lounge. The cool night air hits me as we step outside, and I breathe in a freshness from the thick air of smoke. He unlocks his car, a sleek black sedan, and opens the door for me.

As I slide into the passenger seat, I can't help but feel a thrill of anticipation. He eases into the driver's seat, and we pull off into the night, the city lights blurring past us. I know what's about to happen. He doesn't and it gets me excited.

"Would you like something to drink?" He asks as he steers smoothly down the road. "I got some wine coolers in the trunk."

How old does he think I am? Sixteen? "Pull over."

He looks at me once and then twice before bringing the car to a stop. "To get the drink?"

"Nah, I'm not thirsty. So there's no need to go further than this. I need to get back to my car when I want. So this is far enough." I position my body so he can get a good look at what brought him to me. My titties. "You trying to fuck or not?"

He pulls over. "You are very strange, but I like it. So, tell me what you want to happen."

"Why do you cheat?"

He chuckles. "I don't know what you —."

"You a married man, Lewis. You been married to your wife for six years and you have twin daughters. But here you are —."

"You don't know shit about me, bitch!" The smile slides off his face like hot butter.

"Nigga, I just gave you your details. You should be asking me how much more I know. Now answer my question or else."

"Or else what?"

I nod at the gun in my lap. It's been there the entire time, but he was probably too busy looking at my titties to notice. Now he does though.

"Why do you cheat on your wife, nigga?" I repeat.

He moves around, uneasy. "I don't know...I mean I guess I —."

I stab him with the small weapon I was holding on my thigh. He didn't see that either.

"Ahhhh, what the fuck!" He yells out. Blood gushes everywhere and I smile. I like the look of it expanding on his blue jeans. "Fuck is wrong with you?"

"Why cheat?!" I ask again.

"Because I was bored!" He yells holding the gash in his leg. "Fucking bored! And I hate her for lying and making me think life would be fun every day! For making me believe I wouldn't want to look at another woman! Or be happy!"

"Why didn't you do something to make the marriage interesting? Why was it all on her?"

He looks down, holding the gash harder. "It wasn't all on her. I fucked up too."

I didn't realize until I exhaled deeply that I was holding my breath. I was about to take things a step further until my phone rang. Instead of answering in his car I open the car door, still aimed as I back out. "Don't try and follow me."

"Just leave! I have to go to the hospital!"

I slam the car door and he speeds away, almost running over my feet. Only when his rear lights dim do I answer the phone. "What's up, Bambi?"

"Where are you?"

"I'm on my way."

BAMBI

I stand outside Denim's bedroom door, the muffled sound of her crying seeping through the wood. Is this because of me? I came at her hard earlier. But beefing with Kevin put me in a different mood. At the same time what I said was true, about her being weak, but I could've gone at it a different way.

I knock gently, waiting for a response, but when none comes, I push the door open and step inside. "Denim?" I say, trying to keep my voice steady as I close the door behind me. "Chef said you didn't eat."

Denim looks up from her bed, her eyes red and puffy. She shifts uneasily, avoiding my gaze. "I wasn't hungry."

I take a step closer. I'm sorry for how I treated you in the living room earlier. I was out of line."

She sits up, her expression hardening. "Oh, now you sorry? After you and Race made it clear how you feel about me?"

I clench my fists, struggling to keep my composure. "We're all under a lot of pressure. We didn't mean—"

"Don't give me that shit, Bambi," she snaps, her voice rising. "You think I didn't know how you and Race see me?"

My heart aches at her words, but I can't back down. "I'm trying to protect this family. Because if I miss one step...just one... shit falls apart."

"At least you have Kevin!"

"Kevin has me!" I yell. "There's a difference! Listen, I just need you to—"

"To what? Be perfect? Never mess up? Never cry?" She stands up. "I'm doing my best, Bambi. But with Bradley lying to me—"

"All our husbands lie."

"Not like this." She looks down. "I...um...I followed him today and saw him with another woman."

Her confession hits me like a punch to the gut. "Denim, I'm sorry."

"So am I."

"Who is she? Better yet, where is she and I'll have her dealt with."

"So what... another woman can step up? And another after that? If he doesn't want me nothing you do, including killing them will make it change."

"You're right."

She shakes her head, tears streaming down her face. "Everything is falling apart, and I don't know how to fix it."

I step closer, reaching out to her. "Denim, we'll get through this. But first we need to focus on the drones and then we can deal with Bradley. For now, just try to be strong."

She hesitates. "The way I feel, I don't want to be a liability."

"Then don't."

Race enters unexpectedly. "I'm here, what's up?"

"What you got on your face?" I ask. "That stuff you use to wear those masks?"

She picks at a few lines of what looks like sticky string from her cheek. "Oh, nothing. What's going on?"

"I have a plan to discover whoever may be behind the drones. Kevin told me to stand down but I'ma apply pressure on his ass to do something anyway. So I'm gonna call a family meeting. Tonight."

I sit in the living room, watching as everyone sips from their glasses. The staff had just disappeared into the background, leaving us to our own devices. Kevin, Ramirez, and Bradley are here, with Bradley sitting far away from Denim.

I clear my throat, standing up to address them. "I have a plan. And it starts with coming clean," I say, my voice firm.

"Come clean with what?" Kevin asks. "Fuck is you even talking about?"

"We need to put every secret on the table because if I'm right, whoever is behind the drones and the package will be revealed. And we have to do it now before the Kennedy Court unveiling. Before Melo comes home."

Kevin's eyes narrow, and he leans forward, setting his glass down with a thud. "This is what the fuck I'm talking about. Who put you in charge, Bambi? Last I checked, I'm the head of this family."

I meet his gaze, refusing to back down. "You're in charge of product, Kevin. There's a difference. But this is my plan, and whether you like it or not, I'm going to see it executed."

Kevin's face flushes red, and he stands up, towering over me. "After all these years, you still think you can just take over?"

"Why you acting so confused?" Race says. "You know keeping us afloat has always been Bambi."

"Stay out of it," Ramirez says to her.

"Nah, not when it comes to this shit. Because what I won't do is allow y'all to act like it's not true. No Bambi, no stability."

"This family operates under my leadership." I say more firmly to Kevin. "We all know that. And I'm not gonna sit around and let you disrespect. Just because you reminiscing about Bunny."

I see Bradley and Ramirez frown.

"Reminiscing about Bunny?" Ramirez says. "What's that about?"

Kevin ignores him and focuses on me. I guess he doesn't tell his brothers everything after all. About how he fucked that bitch. "You have gotten carried away with—."

I press him harder, almost as if I've been waiting on this moment all our lives. Maybe I was. "You have been trying to replace me since that shit in the Vegas. I haven't said much because I thought that would change. But after all these years I see it hasn't. You don't even want to be in the game no more, nigga! Why should I let you handle the coke business?" I'm so close to him now he has to move. "Secrets, Kevin. Do you have any?" I take a deep breath, standing my ground. "That is what this meeting is about and that is what I want to remain on topic."

He shakes his head. "This is bullshit, Bambi."

"You can call it whatever you want," I say, my voice calm but sure. "But I'm not asking for your permission. I'm telling you how it's gonna be."

"Let's see who is really in charge." He says nodding to his brothers.

Bradley and Ramirez exchange glances before standing up.

"Come on, let's go," Kevin mutters, and the brothers turn to leave.

As they walk out, I begin to pace. If he can't even handle me heading this up, he definitely won't want to reveal his secrets. But I will get the info I need because whoever is targeting us has a personal vendetta.

I'm sure of that shit.

When they disappear, I turn to my girls. Denim's eyes are red, but she looks more composed than before, while Race watches me with a calculating gaze.

"We're alone now," I say, my voice softer. "Them niggas are all for each other. So we can't afford any secrets between us. If we're going to get through this, we need to be united. Even if it's against our own husbands."

"Especially against our own husbands," Race says.

Denim nods, her hands trembling slightly as she sets down her glass. "They not budging. What do we do now, Bambi?"

"Do you think you can get anything out of Bradley? Alone?"

She shakes her head no. "After what I saw tonight, with the other woman, I might not be able to even talk to him without slapping him down."

"What about you?" I ask Race who nurses the bandage around her finger.

"Nah...we not in the friendly mood with each other. Been years."

I scratch my head. Pace in place. *Think. Think Bambi. You have an answer for this. You have an answer for everything.*

I have an idea! I don't know why I believe it will work but I do.

"So we change it up," I say to them both. "You talk to Kevin, Denim. You talk to Bradley, Race. And I'll talk to

Ramirez." I take a deep breath, feeling the weight of the moment.

Race laughs. "What makes you think they'll talk to us?"

"Because they wanna talk to anybody but their wives. They know this moment is important. But they don't want to give me the satisfaction of a win."

Race nods.

"What if they won't talk?" Denim says.

"They will. But if they don't, they don't have to worry about the drones. Because I'll ruin their lives by making things real uncomfortable."

After fifteen minutes of talking to my sisters, I decide to get right on top of things. After all, time is not on our side. We need to find out who's threatening us before Melo comes home, and we need to find out now. Without delay, I walk up to Ramirez, who's sitting on the edge of the bed, looking annoyed. He had something in his hands but puts it behind his back before I could see what.

"What's up, sis?" He says dryly.

"I need you to tell me the things you don't want other people to know."

"Other people?"

"Race."

He laughs once and nods. "I don't know what you think I have to say but nothing is going on with me. If anything, I been here, getting this money and trying to make my marriage work."

"I'm not the police, Ramirez. You don't have to lie or fake with me."

He stands up. "That's the thing I don't get about you. When people don't give you the answer you want—"

I cut him off, "Do you need any reminder of what happened? We had drones fly over this property. Now whether you tell me what's going on or not, I have no intention of going away. My son will be here soon for this unveiling and if he even thinks we still mixed into the drug shit he will cut us off. And I can't have that!"

He sighs and sits down, looking defeated. "I'm willing to talk to you. But afterward, I need you to help me."

I fold my arms against my chest and lean on the wall. "I'm listening."

"I want you to help make things right with Race."

"What's wrong with Race?"

"We don't see eye to eye. Ever since that thing with Carrie."

"The situation with Carrie happened long ago, Ramirez. I know Race isn't holding you to that no more."

"She's not holding me at all. That's the problem. I don't know about you and Kevin, but I miss making love to my fucking wife."

"So go see a counselor!"

"Do you know how hard it is for me as a man to come to you right now? Picture me sitting in front of somebody I don't know. Our secrets are our secrets, and I'm not letting an outsider in on shit."

I take a deep breath. "Okay...okay...I don't know if Race will listen to me, but if you seriously help me right now, I promise I'll do what I can."

He nods. "Okay. There's this woman..."

He wants to tell me about a bitch? I'm annoyed but continue to listen. "Okay. Finish."

"There's this woman who I was seeing from time to time. She owns a school in D.C."

"You dealing with somebody that owns a school?"

"There are a lot of private owners. You don't know that?"

"I do. I just didn't think that you would be fucking one of them."

"Just because she owns a school and is a teacher, doesn't mean she's not a freak. She has a lot of shit with her. For instance, going to swinger's clubs with me and all kinds of shit. She ain't innocent, which is why I like her."

"Then what happened?"

"She wanted more. And when I told her no, she told me I would pay for it. Now there's nothing in me to believe she knows my address, or that she's hard bodied. But I've never seen a woman angrier than I did her, outside of all of you and my wife. So you tell me."

I nod. "Is there anything else?" Ramirez been off lately and looking ashy, so I feel like he's hiding more.

"For me, that's it."

I take a deep breath, absorbing the information. "Thank you for being honest with me, Ramirez. I'll do what I can to help with Race. But we need to stay focused on the threat first."

"Understood."

CHAPTER EIGHT
RACE

I know what I have to do, but I don't want to. I have to speak to Bradley even with our past. A past I wish I could take back. Years ago, before Scarlett was banished, I learned that Ramirez had fucked her so, I slept with Bradley to get revenge. I was over it the moment I was done, but he held onto the feeling a little bit longer.

Our lies went beyond the bedroom. During one of my biggest betrayals, Bradley killed Sarah because she was a snake. Not only to her daughter Denim but to our entire family. And so, after he murdered her, I helped him chop up her body, a secret we shared to this day.

Walking down the hallway, I'm not surprised to see him outside, sipping something brown while staring out at our lawn. I slide the glass door open, close it and then sit next to him. He smiles, probably wondering why he and I are alone.

I never let him be with me alone.

Not anymore.

"You finish looking at them broken drone bits?" He asks.

"Yeah. They were nothing but scraps. Had them burned." I sigh deeply. "What's up with you though?"

He nods at the liquor bottle on the glass table between us. "You want anything to drink?"

I nod, even though I want to keep my wits about me. He reaches down, grabs another glass from underneath the table, and pours me a drink.

"I can have the staff bring ice if you want," he offers.

He acts like he's the only one with a little household power. "I'm good," I reply taking a sip.

"This is new."

I swallow hard. "Don't go there."

"I'm for real. Since when have you been alone with me?"

I shake my head. Things are already tense enough.

"I don't know why you're so concerned, Race. Our secret is still safe. And you better keep it that way. Denim could never handle it." He takes another sip, and this time, I do the same. "The crazy thing is, throughout all of that, it never stops me from loving you."

"You have a whole wife who I happen to care about," I reply, glancing through the glass door into our house to make sure no one is coming. When I'm certain we are still alone, I focus on him again. "You bringing shit up is the reason why I can never be alone with you, Bradley. You won't let it go. Anyway, I came out here for something else."

He looks at me, intrigued. "What is it?"

"I want to know," I hesitate because the words are difficult to release. "I want to know your secrets. Things you are afraid to tell Denim or even your brothers."

"You mean besides what we did and the fact that I love you?" He chuckles, but I don't see anything funny.

"Yes, besides that."

"There is something, something that could possibly be an issue."

"Does this something have anything to do with the bruises on your face?"

He drinks everything in his glass and pours another. "When the drones first flew over the house, I went to somebody I thought may be involved."

"I'm listening."

"That person is Scarlett."

My heart drops. "Scarlett? Fuck you still talking to Scarlett for?"

He shifts a little.

I put my glass down, feeling a surge of anger through my body. "What you doing talking to that bitch? Huh?"

"She got in touch with me a few years after you had her jumped, and she said all she wanted to know was that Master was okay. And I figured my brother would have wanted his ex-wife to know about her son."

"Your brother was done with Scarlett before he died."

"That's not true," he yells. "He may have been done with her in terms of the relationship, but they were still married, and he cared for her. And that's my nephew, and Scarlett is his mother," he points at the house.

"Denim is more his mother than Scarlett will ever be."

"You asked me if I had any secrets, and that's the one. Denim was there the last time I saw her, and I thought she was on to me. I was wrong. But if I were you, I would keep that under wraps because I'm not sure the rest of the girls will be able to handle it."

"Do your brothers know?"

"Of course."

Them niggas stick together like we outsiders. In another country. And Ramirez wonders why I don't fuck with him. Why he ain't tell me this shit? I'm the one she hates more so being loyal to her puts me in danger.

I grab my drink and throw it in his face before walking out.

CHAPTER NINE
DENIM

When I walk to see Kevin, he's with his brothers Bradley and Ramirez. I don't even bother to look Bradley's way. I don't feel like dealing with the lies he's prepared to tell me about that strange woman who hit his car. Instead, as they speak quietly in the kitchen over sandwiches, I hold my head high and say, "Kevin, can I speak with you? In private."

"About what?" My husband asks.

"I'm not talking to you," I respond, focusing on Kevin. "Can we speak alone?"

Kevin looks at both his brothers, and they walk towards the exit. But Bradley touches my arm and I shake it off. He doesn't have the right to touch me. He doesn't have the right to do anything as far as I'm concerned. Because all I know is that I saw him with a white woman in a car, speaking heatedly. A white woman with red hair. So unless he's willing to tell me all the details, he's as good as dead to me.

"Denim, I'm sorry. Can we get past this?"

"You heard her," Kevin interrupts. "She wants to speak to me. Do all that marital bullshit later."

Bradley nods and walks away with Ramirez. I approach Kevin, my anger barely contained.

"Do you know why I'm here?" I ask.

He turns his attention to the sandwich and cuts it. "You want any of this? I make a mean ass stack."

"No, I can't eat."

He turns around for a second and looks me up and down. "I can tell you're losing a lot of weight." He focuses back on the sandwich.

"Not losing a lot of weight, just some."

He puts the sandwich down. His back is to me. He takes a deep breath, then turns around and leans against the counter before crossing his arms over his chest. "You know, next to Bambi, out of all the sisters, I always thought you were the most beautiful."

I don't know what I was expecting, but it definitely wasn't that. "You think I'm the most beautiful outside of Bambi?"

He nods.

"You never told me that before."

"I don't know if that's something you should tell your sister-in-law. I don't know why I'm telling you now except I'm concerned." His hands drop at his sides.

I step closer. When I entered I wanted to fulfill my end of the bargain and speak to Kevin about his secrets. But now I'm more intrigued about his feelings toward me.

"You're letting yourself go, and I know why." He grabbed one of my blue dreads and put it behind my ear. "But I just want you to know the thing that you're concerned about, you don't have to be."

"If you gonna talk to me, Kevin, you might as well be up front."

"I am up front. I want you to get back to who you were. I know you want that too. Don't allow whatever my brother has going on to get in the way of that. Trust me, you don't know what you think you do about him."

He playing mind games. "What are your secrets, Kevin? What are the things that you're holding back or that you're afraid to tell the family? Or even Bambi."

He smiles and turns back around to his sandwich. "She sent you in here to pick my brain."

Silence.

"You can tell my wife that I would have spoken to her tonight in our bedroom after she had my dick in her mouth if she had just waited."

"Nigga, I'm here now! Don't try to play my sister!"

By T. STYLES   90

He laughs a little, takes a bite of his sandwich, and turns back around to face me. "There she is."

"Do you know who may be mad at you and targeting us?" I ask him firmly, and for some reason, I'm filled with strength. Maybe it's the fact that he tried to run mental games, or maybe it's the fact that I don't have anything else to lose. Either way, I'm standing up to the great Kevin Kennedy.

"You know I have another son. His mother was never happy that she didn't get the lifestyle she thought she would by fucking with me. Outside of the little beef here and there on the street, there's nothing else that I can think of that would cause a problem."

"Are you sure?"

"I'm as certain as you are." He winks. "Now, what secrets do you have? And Race and Bambi?" He continues. "After y'all finish with me and my brothers, you need to turn the mirror back on yourselves. Because I can guarantee that what's happening with this family may not have shit to do with us. "

He walks away with his sandwich in hand, leaving me with more questions than answers.

CHAPTER TEN
BAMBI

I wait impatiently for my sisters to come in, my mind racing with every possible scenario. The walls seem to close in on me, the air thick with tension. I need answers, and I need them now.

Denim comes in first and smiles. "Alright, I spoke to Kevin. And I do have information."

I nod. Already she's doing me proud. Next, Race enters, but she looks more intense.

Before Race can speak, Denim says, "Before we talk about what they said, I need to talk about us first."

I look at her and fold my arms over my chest. "What about us?"

"Do any of y'all have any secrets?"

I shake my head. "Kevin got to you, huh?"

She glares. "Like I said, Kevin and I spoke, and I'll tell you what he said after this question is answered. Do y'all have any secrets that could've caused what's happening to occur?"

I think about my life. I've been involved with another man for nearly five years. The situation with him and I is unique. We don't speak. We don't talk about our past. I text him a time. He confirms yes or no. And we meet up in the same place, once a month. After we make love, he holds me and leaves.

It's perfect.

He doesn't ask me how my day is, and I don't ask about his. And I will say this: it is the most romantic thing I've ever experienced outside of when I first got with Kevin. But clearly, he's not an obstacle. So I say, "I have nothing to hide."

I look at Denim. "What about you?"

Denim shuffles a little.

"Denim, you asked the question, so do you have an answer? Do you have anything to hide? Do you have any reason to believe that whatever happens to us behind those drones is related to your shit?"

She takes a deep breath. "Yes."

Wow. I wasn't expecting that. "Okay. What's going on?"

"I've been having someone follow Bradley. And at first, the person was following him and giving me good information. But when he learned who we were, with the drugs and all, he wanted more money. And started saying he would go to the police and leak information before

Melo's unveiling. At the same time, I think he was selling our shit to someone else."

"Oh my God," Race says under her breath.

"I paid him what I could, but he always wants more."

"So this nigga blackmailing you?" Race says.

Denim nods.

"Greedy ass, bitch," Race yells. "We could've dead-ed his ass a long time ago had we known! Why you ain't tell us?!"

"Yeah, this mothafucka definitely top of the list," I say.

"I don't wanna keep hashing over this issue. I'm being honest. So we can do whatever we gotta to him because he may be the fucking reason. I just don't want to hold anything back from both of you."

I think about the dude I fuck on the low and decide I may have to pull him up after all. Because Denim does have a point. She is coming clean so the least I can do is check my situation for snakes.

I take a deep breath. "If this detective fucks up my son's real estate development deal I'm going off."

"Me too," Race says.

I look at her. "What about you? You got any secrets?" Race looks down and back up. "Race, you have any secrets or not?" I persist.

"No, nothing."

"So I'm the only one who got shit to come clean about huh?" Denim says.

Race and I look away.

"I don't have nothing else I can think of," I say.

"Me either," Race responds.

I nod and my focus returns back to the men. "Okay. So I'll start first. From my conversations with Ramirez, everything seems to be clean except..."

Race frowns. "Except what?"

"He been fucking with some lady who owns a school."

Race shakes her head. "Yeah, I know about that bitch."

"You...you know about her?" I yell. "Why you ain't tell us?"

"Because—."

"You don't care what he doing on the side," Denim says finishing her sentence.

"I don't. As long as he stays away from me, I'm good."

"Wow," Denim says.

"This nigga does all he can to get my attention. So he keep resorting to high school antics he believes will work. Trying to get me jealous. Like this one time he took me to the movies and spent ten minutes flirting with a female next to us while the movie was on. You know what I did?

Offered her some of my popcorn. It sent him through the roof. He stormed out and everything. So trust me when I say I'm done with his ass."

"Fuck is wrong with him?" I yell.

"Exactly!" Denim responds.

"It's fine," she says. "So what about you? Have you learned anything from Kevin?"

Denim crosses her legs. "Kevin tells me outside of his baby's mother —."

"The boy is grown now." I interrupt.

"Well he says outside of his son's mother, he doesn't have any enemies either."

"It can't be her because Kevin been pushing money into a private fund for that boy," I say. "Plus she ain't got enough money to send a rack of drones and shit. But we'll check her to be sure."

"You all are not going to like what I have to say," Race says.

I frown, my heart rate kicking up. "What you talking about?"

"Bradley...um...Bradley been in contact with Scarlett."

It felt like the room was spinning. "What you mean Bradley been in contact with Scarlett?" I yell.

"He's been letting her find out information about Master."

Denim raises her head. "That was the redhead I saw."

"You saw him with Scarlett?" I say.

"I didn't know who she was at the time, but it all makes sense now."

I glare. "This nigga playing us! Fucking playing us! And why the fuck you seem so relieved, Denim?"

"Don't you get it? It wasn't another woman," she says happily. "He was meeting up with her for Master."

"I'm glad you happy," I say, "But it's obvious if she finds the need to sneak behind our backs, then she's willing to do anything. I mean why she ain't come to us? It's not like she ain't fuck Ramirez. How you know she ain't fucking him too?"

"Bambi, don't go there," Denim says.

"It's true!"

"Exactly," Race says.

"Look, I'm glad you so happy and giddy, but that bitch just became number one on the list."

I go to my closet and pull out my fatigues and my white t-shirt. I haven't worn these in a long time, but today feels like the day. The fact that Kevin and them niggas were in connection with Scarlett and we didn't know burns my soul in ways I can't even explain.

Of course, she's involved in this drone shit. What I hadn't stopped to realize was that they were involved too.

After laying out my clothes, I take a shower, letting the water run down on my wet and wavy weave. When I'm done, I towel dry everything and put it up into a bun on top of my head. I lotion my skin and look at myself in the mirror.

That's one thing about getting money. Unless you're doing it the right way, it never seems to bring you peace. You're always on edge. Somebody always wants something. And now, is no different. If Melo wasn't involved, I would love this shit. Handling scenarios is what I do best. But I had something to lose. The worst situation for a drug dealer to be in.

Sliding into my clothes, I'm preparing to head out when my phone rings.

I glance at the screen and see Melo's number. My heart swells and I answer quickly.

"Hey, son," I say, trying to sound cheerful.

"Mom, how you been?"

"Good…we all are. Just waiting on you."

"Everything good on my end but I'm not gonna lie, the Kennedy Court development been on my mind. I just hope I don't mess it up."

"You won't, son. This is your moment."

"This is our moment."

I smile, but he's wrong. He deals in buildings. I deal in coke. There's a difference. "I'm so proud of you, Melo. You've worked so hard on this."

"Thanks, Mom," There's a brief pause before he continues, "I'm bringing a surprise when I come home. Something I think you'll love."

My curiosity is piqued. "A surprise?"

"Yeah, but, Mom," Melo's tone shifts, becoming more serious, "I need you to promise me something."

"Anything. What is it?"

"I need you to promise that you're not doing anything illegal. I know how things been in the past, but this is important to me. Kennedy Court is important to me. I want it to be a fresh start for all of us."

My heart aches at his words. I know the life we've led has been far from clean, and it won't change any time soon, but I also know how much this means to him. "I promise, Melo," I say, my voice steady. "We're good on this end. This is a fresh start for all of us."

"That means a lot to me. I love you."

"I love you too, Melo. More than anything."

We end the call, and I take a deep breath before meeting Denim and Race in the hallway. To do all the illegal shit I told him I wasn't on. "Y'all ready?"

They nod.

We quickly head to the basement where we know Kevin and his brothers would be. I rush down first, and they follow me.

"What the fuck is wrong with you?" I ask Kevin, but I'm talking to all of them. "Why would y'all allow Scarlett back into our fucking lives?"

"Hold up! Come easier with me, Bambi." Kevin says shaking his head.

"You allow this bitch back in or not?"

Ramirez looks down, but it's Bradley who chooses to speak. "My brother would want his son to be in contact with his mother. So we felt it was best."

"It's not only the fact that you're in communication with her. But that y'all didn't tell us. Y'all niggas didn't even bring up her name!" I yell.

"Scarlett is not a gangster," Bradley says. "She ain't have nothing to do with those drones."

"You know her that well?" Denim asks. "That you can be so sure?"

"I'm sure he does. He probably fucked her like Ramirez," Race says.

"Hold up. Where's this going?" Kevin says. "Because what y'all on is not what the situation is about."

"How can we trust any of y'all?" I continue. "Once again holding things back brings confusion."

"Well maybe you not holding the family together like you thought you were."

I'm so mad I could peel his face off.

"A real leader would never have moved like this, Kevin. Ever! Fuck wrong with you?"

"Watch how you speak to me, Bambi." Kevin looks down, then stands up and gets in front of me. "I'm your husband."

"Then act like it, nigga!" I say.

"You need to be taken down a peg or two, Bambi. You have my last name, not the other way around."

"And just how do you think you gonna bring me down a peg?"

"Anyway I gotta."

"Wow," Race says. "He threatening violence against a killer?"

"You want me to be submissive so badly. Well guess what...that will never happen." I walk away from him and directly up to Bradley. "What's her address?" He stuffs his hands into his pocket. "Bradley, what is her mothafuckin' address?"

"I don't know."

"Wait, so you been meeting with her and you don't even know where she lives?" Denim questions. "You ain't even try to find out?"

"We all did," Kevin says. "Even ran her tags."

"Nothing came up," Bradley says.

"How did you even run into her then?" Denim asks.

"One time she saw me while I was at this bar. She walked up to me, crying and in hysterics. To be honest, I don't even know how she found me. But she did. At that point, she told me she missed her son. And I thought about my brother and felt it was the right thing to do."

I'm so angry right now, I could scream. He meeting with an enemy. An enemy who I'm sure would love to put us all away. "You brought her into this family by giving her information on Master. And it's gonna be up to you to find out where she is."

"Who you talking to?" Bradley says with an attitude. "I don't take orders from you."

"Nah, who the fuck are you talking to?" I yell back. I look past him at Kevin and then Ramirez.

When Ramirez stares too hard Race moves to my side.

"So this is how it's going down, you got less than 24 hours to check them niggas on the block to see if any more details come clean on this package being returned, Kevin."

"She really going," Ramirez says under his breath. "Bro, you gonna let your wife talk wild?"

"Stay out of it," Race demands.

"Y'all really don't know me or know what I'm capable of." I say. "I will do whatever I have to do to protect this family, including laying down a few brothers in the process."

I walk away, and without hesitation, my sisters follow.

CHAPTER ELEVEN
SCARLETT

I sit in the back of the club, the lights shining lightly on me, leaving me mostly dimmed, which I prefer. I'm wearing a black low-cut top, leather pants, and red high heels to match my hair. I smoke on a hookah, and every so often, the luminous fog obscures my face.

My best friend, Electra, dances next to me, spinning to the latest song. Every now and again, she nudges me, and I smile, but my attention is elsewhere.

When a man approaches from the right, I get uncomfortable. We paid for the entire area, so technically, he shouldn't be anywhere near the ropes. After a while it becomes obvious. He's trying to get at Electra's fine ass. "How you ladies doing?" He asks.

Electra winks and flashes a smile. "We doing good. You got any plans to make it better?"

He grins. "You fine as fuck. That's one of the reasons that brought me closer. Finding out you have a personality too is a win."

"How can we help you?" I ask, my tone dry and cold.

"I just wanted to know if I could buy this young lady a drink," he says, looking at Electra.

Electra grins and pinches his cheek. "That's all you want?"

I add, "After all, we already got bottles over here for days."

The man's eyes fall on the liquor, and he nods. "It was just a gesture. But can I get your number?" He asks Electra.

Electra whips her pink hair over her shoulders, dips into the pocket of her skin-tight jeans, and grabs her phone. "Let me get yours instead."

When she finishes, she sits next to me. "What's wrong with you? You used to be fun but now you dry. Tell me what's going on in your mind so I can understand."

"It's about Master. I'm tired of waiting. Are you ready?"

"So we really going through with this?"

"After I hit his car and didn't see the pictures of my boy, it makes me want to go off plan."

"But I thought you got Bradley's phone."

"I can't get in it."

"You want me to have somebody try?"

"Nah, I'm going to hit up Richie Rhodes later. I don't know how he does it, but he has a knack for getting into them phones. But are you ready? I mean really ready. For the next part of my plan."

She turns her body so she can look directly into my eyes, pushing my red hair back behind my ear she breathes deeply. "I have been telling you over and over to let this go. Besides, you already got one up on them that they don't even know about. You winning, even though you can't see it."

"Until I get Master, I'm never winning." I stare harder at her. She looks compromised. "You getting too close?"

"No."

"Are you sure? I mean, no matter what, will you choose me, Electra? Or are you gonna fuck me over like everybody else in my life?"

"I'll choose you. Always."

"Good, then stay ready."

CHAPTER TWELVE
BAMBI

When I exit the shower, I'm annoyed to find Kevin awake. He always sleeps in late. As if he doesn't have a care in the world. "We need to talk," he says.

"So you finally want to talk to me?" I respond, glancing to my right.

I see that bunny rabbit and walk back into the bathroom to grab a clothes hamper because I have a plan for that bitch. I know I look dumb because I haven't washed our clothing in years. We hired someone for all that. At the same time, there's no way I'm going to allow that thing to sit in my house, knowing he, for whatever dumb ass reason, feels connected to it because of his aunt.

"Bambi, I understand we have to find out what's going on," he says.

"I don't think you do," I say. "You talk to me like shit in front of them niggas."

"Well the way you been moving makes me believe you think I'm not man enough to take care of this family."

"Since when does being man enough mean you have to be rude as fuck?"

"Cut it out," he snaps, his voice sharp. "You were the one talking about murdering me and my brothers. So how you sound?"

"I'm asking for real," I say sternly. "If you want a wife who will cook and clean, I'm not her, Kevin. I thought you knew that."

His feet are planted firmly on the floor, and his hands are now clasped together. "I respect you and I love you, but you move off a different space than I do when it comes to this street shit. You like having meetings when I say we play things by ear."

"Kevin, at some point you have to make some noise. And I do meetings to get info before executing." I point to myself. "Because in order to attack we have to know our opponents."

"I know you. You want to hit five or six people, five of which may not even be involved. And what does that do? Put targets on our back and keeps us in a war longer. I know the drone shit was related to the streets and so I'm gonna get some answers." He walks toward me. "And I never said you were dumb, Bambi."

"That's how you make me feel. You don't treat me like your wife unless I'm fucking you," I yell. "You haven't treated me like your wife in a long time. It's like if we're not talking about business, we not talking. And I'm tired of it."

"So what do you want to do? Go on vacation?"

"I want you to be honest with me. That's all. That's it. And hold me like you love me instead of banging me into a wall or this bed when you want to get off."

"Are you kidding me? You the most beautiful woman I've ever known. If I fuck you it's because of that. I can't keep my hands off you."

"And Denim is the most beautiful woman too, right?"

His eyes widen. I can tell he wasn't expecting that.

"I know what you said to her in the kitchen."

He shakes his head and smiles. "I didn't mean it like that. You know I'm not interested in that girl."

"It doesn't matter. It's still disrespect. And the fact that you thought using her beauty would get in her head shows you really don't understand women. Or friends."

"Bambi, let me handle the shit on the streets. Stay out of it."

"Oh, so we not talking about our marriage no more? The comment about Denim got you off topic?" I laugh. "Nah, nigga, I'm handling the situation on the streets. You stay tucked in and safe at home. I have it all under control."

"You mean like you took control when our son was murdered?"

That hurts, and he knows it. Yet he chooses to destroy me on purpose. "I can't believe you just said that shit. Noah getting killed was not on me!"

"Why not? You were handling things when our son was murdered. That was a fact."

"Kevin, you were just as involved as I was. It's true, the Russians took Noah and every day I have to live with that. But when you stepped out of our marriage and had another son, I stood by you. Never left your side. Despite the vow we made. And now you gonna stand by me or else!"

"You stood by me because of the money and the lifestyle, Bambi. Don't for one second believe that it was any different."

He walks out and I'm pissed.

I immediately grab the hamper and toss that stupid ass bunny inside. It was sitting on the windowsill as if it was real. What the fuck was wrong with that man?

On the way to the dumpster I run into Ramirez.

"Have you talked to Race yet?" He asks. "About our marriage."

"I'll speak to her, but I told you we have to wait until all of this blows over, Ramirez." What he doesn't know is that

By T. STYLES 110

she done already told me and Race that she done with his ass. I just don't have the heart to tell him yet.

"That wasn't the agreement. I told you my secret, and you said you would speak to my wife. Listen…" He moves closer. "I heard you in there arguing with my brother. Y'all's thing may be dead, but I'm still fighting for mine."

"Give me some more time," I say. "Because for real, you don't have a choice."

I walk away, not knowing that the bunny fell out and onto the floor.

MASTER

Master just finished eating breakfast. Although normally everybody took care of him, he noticed over the past couple of days that people seemed to ignore him greatly. He was a kid, and there weren't many things that bothered him, but loneliness was one.

The other thing that wrecked his young mind at times was not having Denim's attention. She had seemed preoccupied, and in turn, he spent more time with his redheaded nanny, a woman who although meant well, he didn't necessarily like. She was from

Croatia, and her attitude was stern, but they trusted her after vetting her many times. So, lately she was all he had.

The other thing he loved was paintballing.

Normally Bradley would be his paintball competition, but even he had been too busy lately to take him to the fields. Walking down the hallway, going to his room, he was shocked when he saw the blue stuffed bunny on the floor. He didn't play with toys, and since he was the only child in the house, he figured no one else played with them either. So who did it belong to? Picking the stuffed animal up, he took it to his room and sat it on the chair directly across from his bed.

Suddenly he had an idea.

Grabbing the paintball gun, he aimed at the bunny. Looking through the scope, when he had the bunny in his sights, he fired directly into it over and over and over, loading the bunny with red paint. Red splatters were everywhere, even his furniture, but this wasn't odd as everyone knew how Master rolled. Besides, they had enough money for a cleaning crew, so no matter what he did, the maids would wipe things back to order before night's end.

Although aiming and slaughtering the stuffed bunny seemed innocent, in his mind it wasn't. It was almost as if he was trying to get revenge. Revenge for being ignored, revenge for feeling like a kid and revenge for not having a mother and father's love.

After refilling the paint gun, he repeated the process.

CHAPTER THIRTEEN
BAMBI

I'm standing in the boardroom with Bradley sitting at the table. Denim sits across from him, and Race stands next to me. We may hold their last names, but as of right now, that was it.

I step closer because he's wasting time. "I need you to explain again what it is you do when you meet that bitch, Bradley."

He sits back. "Like I done said, at first it was once a year, but I would take her videos of Master. He's playing in the videos or talking. Sometimes I even get him to say a few words if he's in the mood. But lately she been begging for more. Like suddenly the yearly visits weren't enough."

I shake my head. "And exactly who does he think he's saying these words to?"

"Master never knows. He doesn't care. The only thing he wants is for me to take him to paintball after which I always do."

"So you blackmail the child into companionship for a video?" Denim says.

"Let's not forget he is my blood. You get what I'm saying? My blood is literally running through that boy's veins. So I could never guilt him into anything. I love him."

"Bradley, you're full of shit," I say. "What do you do with the videos? Do you send them to her after y'all meet? Email them?"

"Nope, I just meet up with her," he says, "because she doesn't like links, doesn't trust them, says that links can be used to crawl through your computer and find information. So she demands that I show her the videos in person."

"Demand? On what ground can she make a demand?"

"I mean requests that I meet her."

"So she's not keeping any of them?" I ask.

"Not a one. She looks at them, and from them, she knows he's okay."

"Like she's a good mother," Denim says. "Or are we gonna forget that she abused her own daughter, her firstborn. Now all of a sudden she cares about this one?"

"You say 'this one' as if she's still not his mother," Bradley says. "We can't go around pointing fingers. I fuck with all of y'all, but neither one of y'all did a good job raising your own kids."

Denim is heated I can tell. But I know the Kennedy's are known for zesty ass mind games. So I knew then he was no better than his brother Kevin. "After you let her see the videos, then what?"

"We schedule another time to meet."

I nod. "Okay. So that's what you're going to do now. Schedule the meet."

"There's something else," he says.

"Of course there is," I say. "What is it?"

"She has my phone. My second phone, the one I use for the blocks. When she hit my car, she took it."

I'm so angry I'm dizzy. "You let this woman hold your phone knowing that she could use whatever in it against us?"

"She'll never be able to get into that phone. It's encrypted. Trust me."

"So because of it, she hasn't seen the videos she usually does? Of Master."

"Exactly."

I nod, feeling better now. "Okay, this is what we gonna do. You gonna call her right now and you gonna set up a date for next week."

"And then what?"

"We gonna track her."

"But I just said she doesn't accept links."

"Call her."

He shuffles a little and picks up the phone.

"Speaker," I say.

"I'm already on it."

After what sounds like forever, suddenly we hear Scarlett's voice in the air. And I can't lie, hearing her makes me remember better times. Unlike whatever she had with Denim and Race, back in the day I really loved this girl and wanted her around. I even talked to her after I found out she had sex with Race's husband. In my mind it was sisters before misters. But apparently not everybody could get over it and so Race did what she felt she needed by having her beat down.

"Who is this?" Scarlett says.

"It's me, Bradley. Calling from my other number."

She hangs up and then calls back.

"What's that about?" He says.

"I want to make sure I'm not recorded."

He takes a deep breath. "You were wrong for what you did."

"You mean I'm wrong for smashing in your car after you lied to me? And accused me of dumb shit."

Silence.

"When you hit my car I could have been seriously hurt."

"You got money to get it fixed. Your bones too." She paused. "So Bradley, I don't give a fuck."

"This bitch trying me," I say under my breath.

"So what do you really want from me?"

"I'm calling to keep the promise I made to my brother."

Silence.

"Scarlett, are you there?" He asks.

"I'm here."

"So you want me to keep my promise or not?"

"I don't trust you."

We all look at one another.

"This has never been about trust between us. I told you from the gate I don't like you and you don't like me either." I see Denim smile. "This is about my brother and him wanting to make sure that boy's mother knows he's good. Nothing more. Oh...I would like my phone back too."

Silence.

"Scarlett."

"Yeah!" She says with an attitude.

"We good?"

It seems like forever, but she says, "When do we meet?"

"Next week. Early Tuesday?"

"I got someplace to be on Tuesday. Let's do Monday."

"Monday it is." She paused. "And Bradley, if you're playing games with me, I'll hurt you."

Me and my sisters look at one another. If he don't put her in her place he dead to me! I might even put a bullet in him myself!

"The next time you say something like that to me, I'ma smack the shit out of you. Never disrespect me again."

"Understood."

He ends the call.

"And you say that bitch ain't no gangster?" I say. "Because she sound hardcore to me."

CHAPTER FOURTEEN
KEVIN

*A*s the brothers continue down the street, a tense energy permeates the air. Although they are heavily involved in the drug business, they don't usually engage in hands-on work. They had to admit that they relied on their wives more than anything else and the discomfort they felt showed. And yet, here they are, being forced to take action themselves on the streets.

Their mission is clear…find out why someone snatched the cocaine and gave it back. Or else risk Bambi getting involved. This would ultimately tell all of D.C. and the surrounding areas who was really the boss, something Kevin couldn't have.

When they finally reach Ramirez's set, Kevin parks the truck. "Okay, Ramirez, go speak to Aaron and find any information you can about what happened," Kevin instructs.

Bradley chimes in, "Even though he's done this before?"

"Exactly, because if it was going to be this, we could have stayed home. Why show our faces and risk our lives?"

"I know why he wants to do it again," Ramirez says. "Because he's afraid his wife is harder than him."

Kevin wanted to yoke his throat. "You sound scared."

"I'm not scared," Ramirez continues. "I'm just saying I thought we were gonna do something different at this point."

"Bounce," Kevin says.

Ramirez shakes his head and slides out the passenger seat and approaches Aaron. Although Aaron is outside no less than twelve hours a day, what Ramirez and the brothers like about him is that he's smart. He even takes college courses online to ensure that everything he does, including handling his soldiers, is done with analytics in mind.

"What's up, man?" Aaron greets Ramirez as he pulls him in. "Do you want – "

"I'm not here for all that." Ramirez looks back at his brothers and then Aaron. "I know we talked about this already, but did you find out anything else? About the returned package?"

Suddenly, a few more men start to emerge from the corners of the apartment building. Not feeling comfortable, Kevin quickly exits the truck, and Bradley follows closely.

"No, man. Like I told you when it happened, they took it right when you delivered it, and a couple of days later somebody gave it back," Aaron explains. "I wanted to do the honorable thing and let you know."

"Honorable thing? We were charging you for the loss. How do I know you didn't return it so you wouldn't owe?"

"Because I wouldn't do that," he pauses. "I feel like you want me to say something else. But I don't know any more information. I promise to God if I did, I would come to you about it."

Kevin, Bradley, and Ramirez are so focused on Aaron and the men coming from the darkness that they don't see a pregnant girl with long braids approaching their ride with a bat until it's too late.

WHAP! She hits Kevin's truck, causing everyone to jump and grab their weapons.

"What the fuck is wrong with you?" Bradley yells.

WHAP! WHAP! WHAP! She hits it three more times. Losing his cool, Kevin rushes up to her and takes the bat, shoving her to the ground. Her pregnant belly pointing up in the air.

"Hold up, man," Aaron says. "She pregnant."

"Fuck that shit!" He points at him and then looks at her. "Why you hitting my shit?"

Several men move closer to the brothers, and Bradley makes it clear, "If anybody makes another mothafuckin' step, it's off with your head." His weapon aiming their way. "Don't forget who the fuck we are!"

"No lies," Ramirez adds.

Kevin focuses back on the girl. "What the fuck do you want with us?"

"You killed my son's father. You killed him for nothing," she cries.

Kevin is confused. "What you talking about?"

"Why you have to kill him? He was a good father. He was taking care of me and my son. And now we don't got nobody," she weeps.

Kevin looks at Ramirez, and Ramirez looks at Aaron. "What she talking about?"

"You heard her. We murdered the nigga who was on the package. And four others too."

"Are you telling me you killed five of your own men?" Kevin asks.

"Yeah," Aaron shrugs. "Pretty much."

"Why would you do that shit?" Ramirez questions. "I thought you said you didn't know anything about the return package."

"I didn't. But at the same time, I had to go with the person that gave me the most creeps in my crew and who laid eyes on it when it was dropped off. So it was him."

Kevin drags a hand down his face. "It's thirty-two niggas out here, and not one of y'all can handle business without murder? That's the last resort, man. Not the first."

"I hear what you saying, boss," Aaron says. "But y'all niggas rich. We civilian dope dealers out here. If the package goes missing, we in trouble. I mean Ram made me pay it off until it came back."

Kevin shakes his head. "Let's bounce," he says to his brothers.

Kevin helps the girl up and tosses her bat across the parking lot. "I'm gonna let this one go. But if you ever do some shit like that again, the same shit you did to my truck, I'm doing to your face."

She weeps as the Kennedy Kings pile into the truck and pull off.

When the brothers are five minutes away from their destination, Kevin finally chooses to speak. Ram is seated in the back seat towards the right door, and Kevin adjusts the rearview mirror to look at him.

"Who gave that order?" Kevin demands.

Ramirez shakes his head. "I don't want to talk about it right now."

"I'm not playing with you," Kevin yells. "That nigga took out five men off an order I didn't know shit about."

"To be fair, you don't handle that part of the business remember?" Bradley interjects.

Kevin looks at him, frowning. *"What you talking about?"*

"Listen, when we came back all those years ago, we made things clear. The girls were to handle the streets. We were to handle the product."

"And I'm still trying to find out who gave the order," Kevin continues.

"Race," Ramirez finally admits.

"You mean to tell me that Race told you to kill five people?"

"Yes." He shrugs. *"I mean, why are we so shocked?"* Ramirez says. *"Something happened so niggas had to know we were serious. So I moved."*

CHAPTER FIFTEEN
RACE

I don't know why going out in disguise works for me, but it does. I realize part of the thrill is that for a couple of hours, no one knows who I am. If someone took a picture of me, they wouldn't say, "Is that Race Kennedy of the Kennedy Kings?" I could be solo. I could be somebody else. I could for a moment at least, not be the married woman everyone expects me to be. And I could not be connected to a man I'm starting to hate.

I'm getting ready to lay my prosthetics on my face for one of my secret runs when the door opens. Why do people do that? Come in without knocking. But I'm shocked at who I'm looking at.

Kevin enters and stands by the door for a moment. "Do you know this is the second time I've been near your lab?"

"Second," I respond. "I don't remember a first."

He walks in and looks around, picking up bottles of glue, paint, and anything he can grab. "This is amazing. I knew you did your thing but all of this...the products...the goop...I guess it takes a lot to do what you do huh?"

"Why do I feel like that's a slight?"

"It's not."

"So what brings you in here now, Kevin? You want me to make you a tattoo? A new face, a new chest, a new body?" I ask.

"Can you make me a new life? Without all this bullshit popping off every few years." He laughs. "Nah, I'm good on any of your little creations though."

"I bet you are."

He steps closer. "Did you give Ramirez an order to kill five niggas?"

I glare. "What you talking about?"

"You're smart. You heard me the first time. Did you give him an order or not?"

"Kevin, I don't know what you're speaking about."

"When product was stolen from one of Ramirez's spots."

I search my mind. "I'm still confused."

"I mean...I know that I agreed with the original plan. That I stay on top of the coke connect, and y'all stay on top of the streets. But now I see where that has gotten us. Nowhere. And it leaves me feeling out of touch with my business."

"Kevin, you have the life you wanted. A wife who niggas would die for. We live in a beautiful home. You got more cars than you can even drive. And I heard your youngest son is in a good private school despite where they live."

"What's your point?"

"Outside of this package that was stolen and given back, where's the problem?"

"You forgot about the drones? Is that not a problem?"

"I don't know. Because I'm too busy thinking about Scarlett and how y'all hid her from us. Maybe y'all brought in a white Trojan horse."

"From what I'm seeing, people don't respect us anymore."

"Don't you really mean fear?"

"Is there a difference?" He asks.

"Kevin, it's not my fault that the streets don't know who you are. And it's not my fault you agreed to a situation we're holding you to. Anyway, why you talking to me?" I shrug. "If you got a problem with any of this, you need to be speaking to your wife."

"No, I don't. If we gonna be business partners, then I'm gonna speak to the woman who gave the order because five men were murdered for no reason. Ram said you gave the okay."

Did this nigga lie on me again? "You know what, I'm busy right now."

"So you saying you don't care?"

"What I'm saying is what I just said. I'll holla at Ramirez later. Now please leave," I insist.

He looks at me. "I see you walking out here in the middle of the night wearing a different face. I see you with different wigs too. The camera takes pictures of most of it whether you know it or not. Where do you go, Race? You hiding something else from us out there on the streets?"

He leaves.

The moment the door closes, my stomach churns. Kevin always acts like he doesn't care about shit. So how would I know he was examining me on those fucking cameras? I do know one thing. I'm not gonna be able to go out tonight, that's for sure.

I got something else to do instead.

So I head to my marital bedroom even though I stay in my own room in the house.

Once inside, Ramirez is stepping out of the shower, a towel wrapped around his body. And for some reason, I feel something I normally don't feel. Lust. I close the door and lock it. Walking up to him, I say, "Ramirez, what is Kevin talking about?"

"You may wanna give me a bit more because I'm confused," he says.

He looks different. Hard. For some reason it's like the first time I'm seeing him. "Did you tell Kevin I ordered a kill?"

He shakes his head and walks to his side of the bed, grabbing the lotion. His back is in my direction. Water beads line the top of his shoulders and I want to dry them off like I used to when I took care of him. There were a lot of things I did for him. Moisturize his skin, please him, cook for him, get him dressed. But when I realized that he could so easily replace me, I was no longer interested in being second place.

In my opinion he went down ever sense.

"I told my brother the truth," he begins, lotioning his body starting with his legs. I normally do his back first. "...that you told me to handle it."

"Handling it and killing people are two different things, Ramirez," I walk in front of him. "You can't put that shit on me! It makes me look like I'm not strategic. Plus if he was smart he would know I would have hired my own killers, not you. Because the only one in this family outside of me who likes being hands on in the murder game is Bambi."

"I think my brother took it the wrong way," he says.

"You sure about that?"

I turn around, preparing to leave. "Don't go," he says.

My hand is on the cold doorknob. "Ramirez, what you want with me?" I turn around to face him.

He stands up and walks toward me. Now he's so close I can feel the heat of his body. His skin smells clean and suddenly I feel dirty. "Can we work this out, Race? I mean…I know…I know I fucked up. But how much longer you gonna break my heart?"

"Like you give a fuck."

He shoves me into the wall but not hard enough to hurt. "Hear me and hear me clear…there is no other fucking woman for me."

"What about the teacher?" I question.

He steps back.

"I been knew about her, so don't get mad at Bambi."

"And I know you do your thing too. I know you go somewhere at night. But to me, none of that matters because even though you come and go, you still my wife. And I'm your husband."

"I don't need a bond right now."

"Do you want a divorce or not?" He asks.

That was a turn of events and for some reason, those words cause me to feel sicker. Sicker than I did when Kevin came and questioned me about where I'd been going at night. "Is that what you want?"

"I want you to be happy. So if you want a divorce, tell me," he says, grabbing my hand.

I snatch away. He grabs it again. Back in the day when he was forceful, I liked it. Now it seems strange.

"Race, stay with me tonight. That's all I'm asking."

"To do what?"

He pushed down my pants, licks a finger and slides into me. It glides easily because for some reason I'm already wet. I'm convinced that a woman's pussy and mind are two separate entities and I hate that shit. Placing his face in the pit of my neck he moans.

"Bae...why you...why you so fucking wet?"

He shoves my pants down to my ankles, lifts me up and pushes his stiff dick into my pussy. In and out he moves until I'm trembling. Taking me to the bed he eases me down and pushes further into me. I wrap my legs around his waist so he can fill me up. A few more pushes and I can already feel myself reaching the point.

"Don't leave me, baby," he begs. "Don't fucking...don't fucking leave me."

I don't speak. I can't. This feels so fucking good I hate that he's about to make me reach an orgasm. But before I know it I'm screaming, "FUCCCCCKKKKKKKKKKK!"

CHAPTER SIXTEEN
DENIM

For some reason, Master is agitated today, and I don't know why. Unfortunately, I don't really care either because I have so much going on. So, I refill his paintball guns, make sure he eats, and then leave him with the nanny.

When I walk to my room, I'm surprised to find Bradley there.

"Hey, how you doing?" He asks.

I close the door. "Everything good?"

He takes a deep breath. "No, not really, but you know what I'm going through. We all going through the same thing."

"You sound like you going through way more than me," I say.

He nods. "Went on the block today. Found out that Race gave the okay to kill five soldiers."

I sit next to him on the bed. "No, she didn't."

He frowns. "So, you calling me a liar?"

"Not a liar. Just correcting you."

"Just because you don't see her doing it doesn't mean it didn't happen. I'm telling you she gave the order."

"For what?"

"For the package that went missing and then came back."

I shake my head. "I want to tell you something about Ramirez, but you may not like it."

He turns his body towards me. "I'm listening."

I want to tell him about what the detective saw when he was following all of them, but I choose not to. I go a different route. "I think your brother may be on drugs. So any nigga that's sucks in toxins speaks toxic shit too."

"Hold up. What you talking about?"

"Okay, you know he broke his leg when he fell off that motorcycle last year. And after that he—."

"He took prescription drugs," he cuts me off.

"At first! But I caught him on more than one occasion smoking something that looks like weed but smells like something else in that cave."

"Fuck out of here." He stands up. "You talking wild about my brother."

"He's my brother too and I wouldn't play games like that." I pull him back down and now his leg rubs against mine.

"How you know for sure, baby? Y'all always out the house."

"But I'm here a lot with Master, and I see a lot. And the few times I saw Ramirez, if he wasn't dealing with that teacher—"

"Hold up, you know about that too?"

"I do," I say. "I mean, I didn't know where he was going until he told Bambi but still. Sometimes he be on that shit so bad, not only does it stink up the hallways, making it hard for the maids to get the odor out, but a few times I caught him walking outback with his dick out."

He drags a hand down his face. "Wow. My nigga going out bad. Like...like he's taking this thing really hard with Race."

Its skip the subject time. "Bradley, why didn't you tell me about Scarlett? That shit fucked me up. I would have never gone at you so hard at the gas station had I known."

"You hate that girl!"

"So that's a reason to lie?"

"No it's not." He looks down. "I really am doing what I can for the family. And my nephew so I chose to keep it a secret. But it won't happen again."

"Is there anything else? I mean, are you fucking her?"

"Never! I swear on our dead daughter."

"Please don't."

He nods. "You right, but it's true." He turns toward me. "Do you have anything to hide from me?"

I think about the detective and decide to change the subject. Me knowing that the drones could possibly be my fault makes it hard to push the issue on Scarlett. For now anyway because I stand by the fact that she's a snake. "Ready for tomorrow?"

"I am. I don't know if Scarlett's gonna go for it, but we'll see."

I want to know more. Like what's she's doing with her life. And is she fucking with a new drug dealer because I saw the G-Wagon. But I feel he don't know enough. "How is she?"

"She's different. Like, really different. Feels dangerous. Back in the day, when I first gave her updates on Master she was quiet, and gradually her energy got darker. Now she feels sinister."

"That's a hell of a word," I say.

"It's true." He takes a deep breath. "It's like she's planning something, but I don't know what." He yawns. "Anyway, you ready for bed?"

I hate that she knows more about us than an enemy should. "Let me jump in the shower."

"I'm gonna make a quick run and I'll be back."

BRADLEY

Bradley stormed into Ramirez's man cave, his eyes scanning the dimly lit room. The air was thick with the smell of something way dankier than weed. Ramirez was sitting in his recliner, a half-empty glass of bourbon in his hand, trying not to look the fuck high.

"Ram," Bradley began, his voice low and steady, "we need to talk."

Ramirez looks up, a forced smile playing on his lips. "What's up? You need something?"

Bradley steps closer, his gaze never leaving Ramirez. "Cut the shit, Ram. Is it true?"

Ramirez's smile faltered for a moment, but he quickly recovered, shrugging nonchalantly. "I don't know what you talking about."

Bradley's patience was wearing thin. He could see the subtle signs, the jittery movements, the too-wide eyes and dark circles. How had he not seen this before? Maybe he didn't want to. "Don't lie to me, nigga!" He warns, his voice cold. "I know you been using."

Ramirez laughs nervously, shaking his head. "Man, you sound dumb."

Not feeling like the games, Bradley grabs Ramirez by the shirt, yanking him out of the recliner and slamming him against the wall. The impact echoed through the room, and Ramirez's glass fell to the floor, shattering on impact. Bradley's face was inches from Ramirez's, his grip tight and unyielding.

"I don't know what you on, but your leg heeled over a year ago. So if you are using, the shit stops now. You hear me? No more lies, no more excuses. Get clean or I'll make sure you regret it."

Bradley held him there for a moment longer, letting the weight of his words sink in. Then he released his grip, stepping back and letting Ramirez slump to the floor.

CHAPTER SEVENTEEN
BAMBI

It's the afternoon when I walk into the room, Kevin is pacing. I already know this is going to be something else. Before I even step inside, he says, "We gotta fucking talk and I have two questions."

"What you wanna talk about, Kevin? Just go straight at it."

"The first question is, can you just be my wife? For the moment." He asks, catching me off guard.

I close the door and walk toward the closet, flipping on the light. "No matter what we go through, I'm gonna always be your wife."

"I'm not talking about on paper, Bambi. I'm talking about right here and right now. Can you be my wife without all the judgment, without all the mouth?"

"So do you want me to be your wife, or do you want me to be submissive? Because there's a difference," I challenge.

He nods. "True. I want you to be my wife."

I take my clothes off and slip on my robe. "I can do that."

Kevin's next question catches me even more off guard. "If we were to walk away from all of this and leave everything in the past...the drugs, the money, and really make this development deal work with Melo, would I still have you at my side when it's all said and done?"

My eyes widen. I look at him, then walk away and back. "Kevin, how come every time things get hard, you talk about leaving? What happened on the corner? Did you handle it?"

"Yeah I did. So leave the street niggas alone."

"Are you sure?"

"Bambi, I'm talking to you about us! And how I never wanted to stay in this shit forever."

"What that got to do with me? And if you feel that way, why not feel that way when things going good? It's like you wait for the worst situation that's happening with us and then make a decision that now it's time to get out. But that's not how it works. You don't get to wake up one day and leave after so many people depend on you for their livelihood. You have to have a plan," I argue.

"We do have one! Melo's plan," he responds.

"That's our son's money not ours! Think about our lifestyle! How big it is! Them buildings will never be enough money for the shit I need! The shit I require!"

"But it can grow into more, Bambi!" He moves closer.

"Never! I'm gonna always want more!"

He swallows and breathes in and out. He takes a larger breath. "Look, can you be my wife if things work out with the development? Can we let it all go."

"Like I said, I will always be your wife."

"I need more."

"Well I need you to hold me. I need you to make love to me. But more than anything, when it comes to the drug business, I need you to stay the fuck out the way." I pause. "Now what is the second question?"

He shakes his head. "Did you take that stuffed animal out of here? When I asked you not to do it."

"Am I in the Twilight Zone?"

"Why do you always say that stupid shit? Nobody seen that show but you," He snaps.

"I didn't touch the fucking toy. But if I did, so the fuck what!" I storm away.

CHAPTER EIGHTEEN
BAMBI

I really wish our husbands weren't present, but I guess they needed to oversee whatever we say to Bradley. So, in our living room is me, Denim, Race, Kevin, Ramirez, and of course, Bradley.

We're going over the plan to meet Scarlett to make sure it goes off without a hitch. Even though Master will be used in some aspect, he isn't in the room at the moment. Besides, what could he do beside ask a bunch of questions, leaving all of us with no answers?

"Okay, so first you're gonna take the videos of Master. Then you gonna see her."

"Bambi, I'm not two," Bradley says.

"I know. I just...I just want to tie all loose ends." I pause. "And when you take the videos to her, you're going to put this in her purse," I show him a small, metallic object. It's a tracker.

"Bambi, I have never been around her purse in any of the times I met up. So it's not gonna happen now."

"Make it happen. Even if you gotta let her see you do it," I clarify.

"Why would he let her see?" Kevin asks.

"Exactly. So, you want me to drop something in her purse, let her see me do it, and then what?" Bradley responds. "How is this gonna get us her location?"

"While she's looking at what you dropped in her purse or even trying to put it in her pocket, you're going to slap this one on top of her car. It's magnetic." I show him the second device.

Kevin and Ramirez sit back, shaking their heads. "Bae, I know I told you I was going to let you handle this..." Kevin starts.

"Then let me," I say.

"I'm just telling you it's gonna be an issue," Kevin continues.

"Whether it's an issue or not, this is what I want him to do. Again, try and drop this into her purse or her pocket. And while she's looking at that, put this one on the roof instead."

Bradley drags a hand down his face.

"You act like you scared of her," Race comments, raising an eyebrow.

"I'm not scared of her. I'm ready."

"Good, what time you meeting her?"

"In a couple of hours," He responds.

"Okay, call me when you're there and when it's done. We'll go from there," I instruct.

"Again, I just want to go on the record to say it's not gonna work," Bradley continues.

"Noted," I reply. "Now go take the videos of Master. We gotta move."

BRADLEY

Master was in his bedroom once again, shooting paint balls at the blue stuffed bunny rabbit. The thing was covered with so much paint that it was hard to see its blue fur underneath. When Bradley entered Master jumped up and put the bunny behind his back.

"What you doing in here?" He asks, his voice defensive.

"What you say, little nigga?"

"What you doing in my room?"

"You don't pay nothing in this house. So this my crib, nephew." He pauses, pointing at the floor. "And I'm in my room because it's time to go. You ready?"

"What am I doing again?" Master asks, a bit calmer now.

"Taking some videos. And I want you to do what you always do. Tell me how your day is, what you feeling...basic stuff like that. Just answer my questions."

"These videos are always so stupid. I hope you not putting them on the internet. Uncle Kevin says never let people see you on tape." Master grumbles.

Bradley laughs. "I'm not putting them on the internet. And you not that special whether you want to believe it or not anyway. Now let's go."

Bradley leaves the room, and Master grabs the rabbit, his paint gun and follows him out the door. Once they're outside in the garage that belongs to Bradley, he opens the car door.

"Sit in the back but keep your feet planted on the ground like we normally do," Bradley instructs.

Master tosses his gun and the bunny rabbit inside on the backseat. The stuffed toy bounces to the floor. The gun remains on the seat.

"You ready?" Bradley asks and hits record.

Master nods his head. "Okay, what am I saying again?"

"First, tell me how school is."

"I hate this question."

He pauses the recording. "What I tell you about talking back?"

"Not to."

"Well, answer the question, nephew." He hits record.

"School is fine. I got a new girlfriend. She's jealous of my old girlfriend, but I tell her she ain't got nothing to worry about because I'll pick the nicest one."

He waves the air. "Stop with all that nonsense. What about your grades?"

"Oh yeah, my grades are good too. I get A's and B's, and sometimes I get a C."

Bradley glares and lowers the phone for a moment. "You shouldn't be getting C's. You smarter than that."

"Hey, this is my video, not yours. Remember?"

Bradley laughs. "My bad. But, uh, answer me this…are you happy?"

"I hate that question."

"Are you happy, nephew?"

"Yeah, I'm happy." He looks down.

"You sure?" Bradley thought he saw darkness behind his words.

"I mean, I have my moments like everybody else, but for the most part, yeah, I'm happy."

"Okay. If you wanted to tell somebody something you care about, what would you tell them?"

"You mean like to my real mother?"

Bradley glares. "Why would you say that?"

By T. STYLES

"I mean, I got four mothers…well, three really…because one of them I never met. So since I never met that mother, I would say – "

"What about your father? You don't want to say nothing to him?"

"Oh yeah, or my father." He nodded. "I would say I'm happy. Sometimes I get sad, but it's not for long because Mommy Denim and sometimes my other moms, they make me happy. And my uncles too. I would also say I like paintball. And that I got enough money."

"Oh, you got enough money?"

"Yeah, whenever I want something, y'all get it. So I'm good."

"So we got enough money and give you some," Bradley laughed.

"Yeah, same thing."

Bradley shakes his head and ends record. "Okay, grab your stuff and come on."

Master snatched his paint gun as Bradley turns around. "Close the car door too."

"Oh yeah." Master shuts the door, leaving the bunny inside.

CHAPTER NINETEEN
BRADLEY

*B*radley was smoking weed as he continued to drive down the street on his way to meet Scarlett. The sun was on high and made his truck sparkle like black onyx under the light. When he looks down and sees his phone ringing, he takes a deep breath and answers.

"What's up?"

"Where are you?" Scarlett demands.

"I'm on my way," he replies.

"You should have been here by now," she snaps.

He frowns, looks at the phone, and puts it back to his ear. "Bitch don't come at me like we together. Are you fuckin' crazy? You been different lately. But I'm the same nigga you once knew and I will bounce your white ass off the concrete if you come at me like that again."

"At some point you gonna have to make good on these threats."

"Scarlett, am I clear? Because don't forget I'm the only one giving you a lifeline to your child. "

"And you don't forget either! I just want to make sure you're not playing any more games."

"I didn't play games the first time. I asked a question and you got bent out of fucking shape. Even then I had the video for you to see your son, and you ended up hitting my car before you saw it."

She laughs. "I did that because you questioned my motives when the only thing I ever wanted from you, or your family is a connection with my son. MY FUCKING BLOOD! And I won't let y'all steal something else from me!"

He waves the air. "Cut all that out. I'm sick of talking. I'll be there in a minute." He hangs up.

Pulling up into the closed donut shop parking lot, he parks his Escalade close to Scarlett's new G-Wagon. Within seconds, she gets out wearing blue jeans, a black jacket and a red top. Her naturally red hair shines brightly under the sunlight as she bounces toward him.

"Where's my phone?" He asks.

Shaking her head and reaching into the back pocket of her jeans she pulls it out.

He rolls his window down and she tosses it into the backseat. Squinting, she notices something odd. "What's that?"

He looks behind himself and sees the stuffed animal. "Oh, Master, for whatever reason, was firing that bitch up with his paintball gun."

She reaches in and grabs it.

"Hold up, what you doing?" He asks as he slides out the truck.

"It's my son's and I...I want it. You want me to pay you for it or something?" She replies.

He shakes his head. "It's actually not your son's, but whatever. You can take it. I don't know why he left it in here in the first place."

She brings it up to her nose and inhales. Pulling it away she says, "Who shot it?"

He walks up to her. "What difference does it make?" He frowns. "Are you okay?"

She was about to cry. Mainly because Master was not only her blood, but he was the only connection she had to Camp, whom she secretly still loved. It didn't matter that he was dead and that they could never be together again. It didn't matter that they fought and weren't on the best of terms before he was murdered. All that mattered was that the child was the connection to Camp and, if she was being honest, the connection to the Kennedy family who, every now and again, she hated herself for still loving.

"Where the video?" She demands, breaking her attention from the toy.

Spotting the black jacket she was wearing, he walked up, hugged her and dropped a tiny tracker in her pocket. "Get the fuck off me!" She yells, pushing him away.

"I was only hugging you because you looked fucked up about the toy." She tosses it in her car. "But fuck it."

"Well I'm fine. Don't touch me."

"Won't happen again," he says raising both hands in the air before walking to her truck. "Trust me."

"Where are the videos?"

Leaning on her vehicle, he reaches into his pocket and grabs his other phone. Scrolling through it, he pulls up the video he made earlier that day. Although he already dropped one tracker with ease, he wanted to place the other on top like planned. "Here it is."

She takes his phone and looks at the video. Listening to what Master had to say places a smile on her face. Her eyes water up as usual as she took in her son's joy.

While her eyes were on the phone, he snaps the small tracker out of view on top of her roof, just like Bambi asked.

"He looks healthy," she says. "I mean…y'all really are taking good care of him."

"Like I told you before, he's blood. Of course, he's going to be healthy and taken care of," he replies.

She opens her mouth and closes it before opening it again. "I…I wish I could be in his life," she says, taking a deep breath. She moves closer. "I'm telling you, if I'm allowed to see him and get to know him, I would do good by you. I wouldn't cause any issues." She places a hand over his heart.

He slaps it away. "He has a mother," he snatches the phone. "I done already told you that shit."

She glares. "I'm his mothafuckin' mother! Me! And I'm not talking about them bitches who still hold your name."

"You saw the video," he says. "I'm gone."

"Me too!"

He eases into his truck and pulls off.

When she gets into her truck Bradley saw her disappear. Turning his music up, he was feeling himself and was about to tell Bambi about his work when suddenly his phone rang again.

It was Scarlett.

"Oh, and Bradley, I tossed those trackers on the ground. You did too much by trying to lay hands on me when we both know I'm not your type."

He felt dumb. "Uh...the videos...I mean...I don't know what you talking about."

"The Kennedy Kings always trying to play somebody. I hate y'all niggas."

From the rearview mirror, he could see her waving. But what he also didn't see coming was Bambi until she rammed into the front of Scarlett's truck, similar to what Scarlett did to him.

He almost got into an accident witnessing everything go down in the rearview mirror. He knew in that moment that Bambi set the whole situation up. It was never just about the trackers. It was about getting a hold of her once and for all.

CHAPTER TWENTY
BAMBI

So what I lied to Bradley and followed him from a far. As Race and I pull up, we know exactly what we want to do. Question Scarlett in person for the shit that went down at the mansion with the drones, and possibly with the returned package. But I wanted to do the shit in the same fucking way she did Bradley. By crashing her shit up!

Who the fuck she think she was playing with anyway?

She moonlighting as a gangster!

I'm the real thing.

So I rammed my pickup truck into the side of her truck, just like she did to him. When I saw her shift in reverse, I jump out before she could pull off and yank her door open.

I tap her window with both guns. "Get out…before I fire this bitch up."

She does.

Standing in front of her I can tell she looks different. She was never happy, but now her eyes hold a lot of pain. They're dark, almost evil. Time has aged her quite a bit, even though there is still a ragged beauty around the edges.

"What you doing around my family, bitch?" I ask as I approach.

Her hand moves toward her hip. She has a gun too, I can tell.

"Oh we pulling weapons now?" I raise mine and fire over her head. "The next one going in your fucking mouth! Drop it!"

She trembles.

"We waitin'," Race says.

She places it on the ground and Race takes it.

"Now, why the fuck you still around?" I tuck my hammers. "Or is it that you ain't got no conversation for us like you got for Bradley."

"You just hit my truck," Scarlett says.

I see Race take a picture of Scarlett with her phone and wonder why.

I step closer. "I asked, why you around my family?"

"Bitch, I ain't going nowhere," she says. "As long as y'all have my son, it'll always be that way."

I gaze around to see how many witnesses are looking. There are two although they don't look directly this way. Had I not had everything to lose with Melo's property, I would've laid her down and hired the best attorneys later.

"Your son?" Race says. "You not no Kennedy no more!"

"Then give me my boy. Let me raise him."

I laugh. "You will never get your hands on Master. And them videos you saw…that will be the last time you see him too."

Her eyes widen. "Bambi, don't do this shit!" Her lips tremble. "I'm begging you not to do this. Yes, I was wrong for hitting Bradley's car, but he accused me of something I didn't do."

"Did you send drones over my house? Did you have anything to do with packages going missing?"

"After all this time you still can't keep shit together huh?" She says. "You always looking for a scapegoat. At some point, Bambi you gonna have to realize the common denominator is you."

Just then, Bradley pulls up before quickly jumping out. "What's going on?" He yells.

"Stay out of it," Race says to him.

"Fuck out my way," he says as he walks around her and comes close to me and Scarlett.

"Bradley, I love you, but I need you to stay right where you are." My hand hovers over one of my guns.

"Bambi, what you doing? You really gonna pull a weapon on me?"

"You my brother. I just want you to stay where you are so you don't catch a hot one because I'm tired of this bitch."

"Man, fuck this shit," he says. He whips out his phone, and I know he's going to call Kevin.

"Did you have anything to do with the shit that been happening around my house?" I ask Scarlett. "And with my business?"

"Please don't take my son away."

"That ain't the question!"

"I don't understand."

"So you wanna fake dumb? Aight, so it's gonna go down like this. Don't come near my family. And like I said, you will never, ever be in Master's life. Especially after what you did with the drones."

"I didn't come anywhere near you, Bambi. And I definitely didn't do anything with drones."

"So why you got the bunny in your car? What was it, some kind of camera?"

"I took it because Bradley said Master was playing with it. And I wanted something of my son's. Now I'm asking you not to tear us apart."

"Stay away, Scarlett. This your final warning. You and I both know what I'm capable of." I turn to leave and get into my truck and Race follows.

Once inside we pull up alongside Bradley who's still on the phone.

"You can get off the phone with Kevin now. I'll talk to him when I get home. Besides," I look back at Scarlett, "I made my message clear."

As I pull off, Race and I look at each other. We sit in silence for a while.

"You believe her?" Race finally says. "That she wasn't involved."

I look at her and then sit back. "I don't know."

"I need to hear you tell me you believe her, Bambi. Or that you don't."

"I don't think she was involved. At the same time, at this point it doesn't matter because she still on her sneaky shit. That's why no one ever trusted her but me."

CHAPTER TWENTY-ONE
SCARLETT

I rush into my house, pacing the floor with the blue bunny splattered with paint clutched in my hand. The thought that this might be the last thing I have of my child makes my blood boil. Bradley set me up again, and I won't let it go this time. I push into my office, ignoring my boyfriend who's lounging nearby.

"Hey, we're about to go out. You want to jump with us from the plane?" He asks.

I brush past him, my mind focused. "Not right now," I snap, grabbing my landline to make a call. Within seconds I hear her voice. "Electra, shit just went down."

"Is everything okay?" She responds.

"No, it's not. But its time. Them bitches hit my fucking truck!"

"Who?" My boyfriend interjects again, and I wish he goes away. "I'm on the phone," I tell him, my tone sharper. I focus back on the call. "Electra, listen, I don't want to hear all the reasons why I shouldn't do what we planned. Just take the flight and do what we went over."

"Okay, let me pack," Electra replies. I hang up and turn to my boyfriend.

"Scarlett, do I need to get my son out of here?" He asks, concern etched all over his face.

Disgust churns in my stomach. Had he been a Kennedy, he would be asking what needed to be done next, not whether or not to run. But he's a civilian, and civilians never understand shit like this.

"Yeah, do that. I may be out of it mentally for a while anyway."

"How long is a while?" He asks, taking a deep breath.

"As long as it takes." I take a knife from my drawer and cut deeper into the belly of the stuffed animal. I feel around inside, ensuring there are no cameras. Satisfied it's clean, I look at him. I'll sew it back up later. "Oh, and can you bring Zayden? I want to speak to him before you go."

He shakes his head and then leaves. A few moments later he brings my son to me. I come around the desk and stoop down in front of him.

His innocent eyes look up at me, and I force a smile, brushing a lock of hair from his forehead. "Zayden, baby, I need to talk to you," I start softly.

"Okay, Mommy," he replies, his voice small and trusting.

I take a deep breath, steadying myself. "I won't be able to see you for a while, sweetheart. But I need you to be strong for me and be good for your daddy, okay?"

His eyes widen with confusion. "Why, Mommy? Where are you going?"

"I'm going to get your big brother Master," I explain, my voice gentle but firm. "He needs me right now, and I need to bring him home. But while I'm gone, I need you to be brave and strong, just like you always are."

Zayden's lower lip trembles, and my heart aches seeing him like this. "I have a brother?"

"We agreed to tell him at the right time," Jonathan says. "What are you doing?"

I ignore him. "Everything will be okay, Zayden. When we are all together. I promise."

But I don't want you to go," he whispers, tears welling up in his eyes.

I pull him into a tight hug, holding him close. "I know, baby, I know. But this is something Mommy has to do. I promise I'll come back for you. Just trust me, okay?"

Standing up, I turn to my boyfriend, my expression hardening. "Get him out of here. Take him somewhere safe. I'll be in contact when the coast is clear."

"What if the coast doesn't clear?"

"Then tell him I love him."

I watch as he takes Zayden's hand, leading him out of the room. Zayden looks back at me, and I force another smile, waving until they're out of sight.

CHAPTER TWENTY-TWO
BAMBI

The moment I walk into our house Kevin goes in on me. He's livid, and a part of me feels for him, but I don't see how he thought anything would be different. "Bambi, what you doing?"

"What you mean, what am I doing?" I remove my earring and walk to our bedroom. He's right behind me.

"Bradley had that shit under control, and I thought the whole point was to put a tracker on her. Based on what you did, you don't have any more information than when we started. You wasted a lead."

"Scarlett was gonna do exactly what I thought she did. Drop the trackers on the fucking ground. I raised her to be smarter than that a long time ago! So for me, when she did that it was all about approaching her directly. I knew it was gonna be one or the other." I walk into the room. "Oh, and I told her she wasn't getting no more fucking videos of Master either."

"That's her son."

I sit on the edge of the bed. "That's funny because we do everything for him. And to be honest, I don't care who she

By T. STYLES   162

is to him." I pop off one shoe. "We at war, and she's the enemy."

"But she once was your friend...your sister. And say what you want can you imagine not knowing what the fuck was up with Melo?"

"Once, I was eighteen years old. Does it change anything now that I'm not?"

He steps closer. "We have a big life. You doing things like hitting a car in broad daylight brings attention to this family. Brings attention to Melo. People know us as respectable. Don't fuck it all up!"

"Being respectful was always your thing. You were the one who wanted out of the limelight, wanted people to think we were legit. Maybe I'm more of a hustler than you ever were."

"Bambi, please slow down. The thing about planting seeds is this...you have to allow time for things to grow. Let's look at the leads we placed out there. We done already talked to Ramirez and his crew. And now you did what you did to Scarlett. We wait a couple of days and if nothing else pops off we know we scared the fuck out of whoever was involved. If something does happen we know it's Ram's people or Scarlett."

I hear Kevin, but I don't care what he's talking about. My plans be my plans. If he wanna go legit and green, that's on him. But I'm not about to fake like I'm some sweet hustler's wife.

I toss my ring to him. "Fuck you! I want a divorce!"

I storm out.

CHAPTER TWENTY-THREE
BAMBI

"You were out of line," Bradley tells me. "I don't care about your reasons."

We're all in the kitchen, messing over dinner since we told the chefs to take off. It's mostly leftover lasagna and some garlic bread, but now, as I look at him over the table of food, I can tell this is about something else, and I'm ready.

"You sound like a parrot on repeat."

"You used me," he says. "You actually had me believing the plan was to do with the trackers."

"I don't trust her. And you don't trust me. You don't even trust your wife."

"Bambi, that's not fair," Denim says.

"I know this is your husband, but when it comes to war and business, you're gonna have to pick a side. And I'm not gonna make you do it in front of him because we both know what the answer will be."

"What does that mean?" Bradley says, looking at me and then at Denim. "Anyway, I don't think she knows."

"What you mean?" I ask.

"I don't think she had anything to do with the drones. Or taking our package and bringing it back. I don't think she's responsible for any of it."

"Not that I believe you but let me hear your theory. Because she had that bunny in her car."

"Wait, the bunny that I had in my room?" Kevin asks. "From the drones is gone?"

"Can you get the fuck over it!" I yell.

"Anyway," Bradley says interrupting me. "When Scarlett saw it in my truck, she asked for it and took it. It was like she was seeing it for the first time."

"So you think just because she didn't know where the bunny came from that puts her out?" I ask.

"I have been meeting this woman for years. And now, all of a sudden, she's into the high-tech operation that was needed for those many devices? It doesn't add up."

"It doesn't matter at this point." I look at my girls and say, "Y'all coming with me?"

Race follows me immediately, but Denim hangs back for a moment before following too. When we are out in the hallway, I say, "We need to leave for a couple of days."

"Leave?" Denim says. "To go where?"

"My place."

"Your place?" Race frowns. "You have a place outside of the mansion?"

"Yeah, y'all don't?" I can tell by the looks on their faces I'm alone. "Anyway we going to my crib. Have your conversation with your husbands but we're gone tonight."

DENIM

The night is thick with darkness, except the only light coming from the dim lamp on my nightstand. Shadows stretch across the room as I stand in front of my closet, pulling out clothes and tossing them into a suitcase. The weight of leaving without my husband for the night is suffocating.

Bradley walks in, confused, I think. "Denim, what you doing?" He asks, his voice tight with worry. "Where you going?"

"I gotta go," I say, not stopping to look at him. I grab a few more items and shove them into the bag, the sound of zippers and fabric are the only noise in the tense silence.

"Go? Go where? What's going on?" His tone is sharper now.

"It's family business, Bradley. Bambi, Race, and I need to handle things alone." I can feel his eyes on me, burning with questions I can't answer.

He steps closer, trying to catch my eye. "Are you choosing Bambi over me?"

I stop packing and look at him, my expression firm. This is a game. A trap. And I realize I need my girls more because if nothing else, he's gonna choose his brothers. "No, I'm choosing the family over outsiders. There's a difference."

His eyes widen, hurt flashing across his face. "Outsiders? Is that what I am to you now?"

I take a deep breath, trying to keep my voice steady. "Bradley, this is about protecting all of us before Melo comes home. To prevent issues. Please understand. Or not, but that's entirely up to you."

He looks devastated, his shoulders slumping. "Fine, but I don't like this. I don't like being kept in the dark."

"I know the feeling," I say, zipping up my bag with a final, decisive motion. "But ain't this what you did to me? Leave without a reason." I walk over to him and place a hand on his cheek. His skin is warm, and for a moment, I feel the weight of my decision crashing down on me. "Just trust me. I'll be back when I can."

"And when's that?"

"When Bambi says so."

He sighs deeply and wraps his arms around me, pulling me into a tight hug. The embrace is both comforting and suffocating. "Be careful, okay?"

"I will. I promise," I say pulling away and grabbing my bag. The room feels colder without his arms around me, but I know I have to do this. "Take care of Master."

RACE

I'm in my lab, tinkering with some equipment to use when we leave, when Ramirez storms inside. "Race, what's going on?" He demands, his voice cutting through the noise.

I barely look up from my work. "What you mean, what's going on?"

He steps closer. "We have to get ready for the Kennedy Court development celebration in a few days. Why you leaving now?"

I finally lift my head, meeting his gaze. "Ramirez, we've been over this. I don't care how much pussy I gave you the other night, we not together." I put my things into a bag and walk past him, grabbing my jacket.

Ramirez reaches for my arm, his touch lingering for a moment before letting go. "Just... be careful, okay?"

I nod, avoiding his eyes. "I'm strapped. So I always am."

CHAPTER TWENTY-FOUR
BAMBI

I lead Race and Denim up to my luxury apartment, a place they had no idea even existed. The building itself is sleek and modern, despite the gritty streets right outside my door. As we step into the elevator, I can feel their curiosity growing.

We reach the top floor, and I open the door to my sanctuary. The apartment is a fully furnished paradise. My floor-to-ceiling windows offer a panoramic view of the city. I chose plush, cream-colored sofas which are arranged around a glass coffee table, and a large, flat-screen TV is mounted on the wall.

The kitchen is separated by a marble island and my chandelier hangs above the dining table, casting a warm glow over the room. Everything in here, every single piece was chosen by me.

Race and Denim exchange glances, clearly shocked. This is a side of me they've never seen, a side I've kept hidden.

"Nice place, sis," Race finally says as she drops her bag on the floor.

"Yeah, didn't know you had it like this," Denim adds, her eyes wide as she takes in the luxurious surroundings.

I nod, but my mind is already focused on the task at hand. "Alright, let's get down to business."

I pull a folded piece of easel paper from my pocket and spread it out on the coffee table. It's a hand-drawn map of our next moves.

"First," I say, pointing to the top of the list, "we're going for Ramirez's teacher bitch. I want to talk to her."

Race rolls her eyes but nods. "I thought we were going to have a little fun but whatever. What's next?"

"We can change the order." I laugh. "But we're going after Kevin's baby mother too," I tap the next point on the map.

Denim's eyes narrow. "You sure that's a good idea? That girl can be a mess sometimes."

"And we not?" I reply. "Finally, I point to the last item on the list. "We meeting up with the investigator."

Denim winks.

"Once we do this, and if we feel comfortable, we sit back and hopefully Melo's function can go on without a problem."

Denim nods. "We with you, Bambi. Anything you need."

"Just one more thing. If y'all hear anything in the middle of the night, leave it alone. That's just me."

The moonlight streams through the large windows of my apartment, casting a silvery glow across everything. My husband called a million times and this time I answer.

"You not divorcing me," he says simply.

"Is that your way of trying to change my mind?"

"Please don't go," he says. "I'll get on my knees when I see you. But we not done yet. We love each other too much for this divorce shit. But for now, I'll leave you alone."

He hangs up.

The moment he ends the call I hear footsteps. Race and Denim are asleep in their rooms, unaware of the late-night visitor at my door. A soft knock echoes through the quiet space, and I move to open it, revealing Lucas on the other side.

I needed him.

Brown skin, neat locs and eyes that I can get lost in forever, he always relaxes me. Mainly because outside of our moment, he doesn't want anything from me.

We exchange no words, our eyes conveying all that needs to be said. His hand in mine, I lead him to my bedroom, the soft light creating an intimate atmosphere. When the door is closed and we're alone, he removes my clothes and I do the same to him.

For a moment, standing face to face, his hands work skillfully, kneading the tension from my muscles as he rubs me head to toe before putting me to bed.

Turning me over, his touch is firm yet gentle, finding every knot of tension and smoothing it away. As he works his way down my back, I close my eyes and let out a deep sigh, surrendering to the sensation. His hands move with practiced ease, and I can feel the weight of my responsibilities lifting, if only for a moment.

"Lucas, do I make you happy?" I breathe out.

He stops massaging me and I miss his touch already. "We talking now?"

"I just want to know the answer. And we'll fall back into silence later."

"More than I can say, for fear you would walk away."

"So you aren't doing anything to blow up my spot? With drones? Fucking with my business? Nothing?"

He rubs my back. "There are a lot of things about me that can be dark, but I would never, ever hurt you."

Nuff said.

That's when the dick enters my greasy pussy. In and out he pushes and my belly sinks into the bed as my ass raises and shoves back softly. The warmth of his body against mine is as comforting as my face pushes against the bed.

No words.

Just a soft passionate fucking.

As the minutes stretch into an orgasm for both of us, I find myself drifting into a peaceful sleep, wrapped in the safety of his embrace. The world outside ceases to exist, and for this brief, precious moment, I am free from any burdens.

Tomorrow, it would be all about that gangster shit.

CHAPTER TWENTY-FIVE
BAMBI

I walk up the cracked sidewalk towards Diane's house, a modest, run-down piece of shit that looks even worse up close. The paint is peeling, and the yard is overgrown with grass and weeds. Kevin's son is in high school, but the resemblance to Kevin is crazy. Just thinking about how this kid was a product of my nigga cheating makes my skin crawl. Race and Denim stay back, lingering by the car parked a few houses down, their eyes scanning the surroundings for any sign of trouble.

I walk up to the fence, noticing how it barely holds together. And I see that Diane is out front, hanging some clothes on a sagging line. She looks up, her eyes narrowing as she sees me approach.

"Hey, Diane," I call out, trying to keep my voice neutral.

Diane straightens up, eyeing me warily. "Bambi. What the fuck is this about?"

I don't answer right away. Instead, I lean against the fence, giving her a long, hard look. "Haven't we been good to you?"

She glares. "Good to me. What you talking about?"

"Have we not been good to you?" I repeat, my tone more insistent.

Diane huffs, crossing her arms over her chest. "Kevin's been absent in our lives for years. It's not enough, Bambi."

I nod slowly. "Kevin doesn't have to be in your life, Diane. But he's good to your son. He makes sure he's taken care of and in a good school. Fucking him was never meant to be a come up for you personally."

She shakes her head, frustration clear on her face. "It's not enough, Bambi."

"Do you want me to pull the stipend? Pushing his ass into public school for this neighborhood?"

"No! Please don't do that."

I step closer, lowering my voice. "Good, so let me ask you straight up. Have you been fucking with my family?"

A sly smile spreads across her face. "Why? What's going on, Bambi?"

I lean in, my voice cold and threatening. "Are you fucking with my family or not? Be careful at how you handle me. Don't let your existence convince you that I'm not dangerous. I keep you alive for that boy. But he's about to be a man now. So what do you think that will make me do to you?"

"No, Bambi. I'm not doing anything to your family."

I look into her eyes. For some reason I believe her. "Good but I'm warning you, Diane. Don't play games with me. If you're fucking with us, it won't end well for you."

She looks down and then breathes deeply. "I'm not involved in your mess, Bambi. Maybe you should look closer to home. Because you look worn the fuck out."

I give her one hard stare before turning and walking back to the car. But I stop, approach her again and slap her with a backhand and then a right. "You and I are not equals. Haven't you learned that by now?"

When I'm done, I walk toward the car and when I reach it, Race and Denim are already waiting, their eyes questioning. "She's not involved," I say, sliding into the driver's seat.

"How can you be sure?" Denim asks.

"Look at this bum house and how Kevin got them living. She's not a threat," I say harder. "And she too broke to buy a threat too."

Denim nods, glancing back at the house. "So what now?"

"We stick to the plan. We still have Ramirez's girl and the investigator to deal with. Let's keep moving. Everything has to be done today before Melo comes home."

Later that afternoon we visited Ramirez's teacher. She didn't give us much of anything useful. She was too scared when we came in to do anything but piss on herself. She wasn't about that life. So, we decided to go see that detective for more answers.

DENIM

The office of Morgan, the private detective, is dimly lit and smells faintly of old leather and coffee. We happen upon his door, and I step forward, my heels clicking on the hardwood floor. Once we're all inside Race shuts the door behind us.

"Not now, I'm busy," he says never looking up from documents he was signing.

"Nigga, raise your head."

Slowly Morgan looks up from his desk, a frown creasing his brow. His secretary, Cherry Downing, is not in the office, as verified before even making our presence known.

"Denim, what brings you here?" He asks, his tone guarded.

"Did you send drones over my home?"

"Drones? I...I don't know what you talking about."

I nod. "I need to see...I need to see the recordings," I say, cutting straight to the point.

"What recordings?"

"All of them. Of you following my husband. And eventually the ones of you following me."

Morgan leans back in his chair, rocking slightly. "I gave you all the footage I had on Bradley. There's nothing left."

I narrow my eyes. "Unless I give you more money huh?"

He smiles. "I have nothing else."

"Prove it. Pull up your computer."

He hesitates, his fingers tapping nervously on the desk. When he doesn't move, I pull out my gun, aiming it steadily at him. "Do it. Now."

Morgan swallows hard and leans forward. He reaches for his computer, taps a few keys and the screen casts a pale light on his face. I watch as he types, bringing up the files. Turning the screen to me he said, "See? There's nothing here. I deleted them all."

I look at Bambi. "I don't believe him," she says.

I focus back on Morgan. "Search for Bradley's name," I demand.

"Look, these are my private—."

Bambi hits him over the head with the butt of her gun and with blood dripping into his eyeball, suddenly he does as I ask, but the search comes up empty. My eyes flick to Bambi and Race again, standing behind me. They nod, indicating I should dig deeper. "Open your picture files," I order.

"On your phone," Bambi says.

Morgan's hand trembles as he clicks through the folders. Suddenly, images of Kevin, Bambi, and the rest of us fill the screen. Bambi and I exchange a look, realizing we've found the rat. He even has photos of Ramirez moving dope on the streets.

"Why do you have these?!" I yell. "Fuck is this for?"

Morgan's face hardens. "I have them because I want to. Because you wouldn't give me the money and you think you untouchable."

"And what the fuck that got to do with these photos?"

"I was gonna sell them to TMZ after Kennedy Court launches."

My grip tightens on the gun. "You don't care who you hurt huh? You know what this means to the family, and you don't care."

He shakes his head, a twisted smirk on his lips. "Not one fucking bit."

Before I can react, Bambi steps forward, her eyes cold and unyielding. "Then why the fuck should we care about you?" Aiming her gun, she doesn't hesitate as a single, sharp shot rings out, and Morgan slumps in his chair, his smirk fading into a lifeless mask.

With him gone to see his maker, the room falls silent.

Race steps forward, her face grim. "We need to clean this up."

I nod, my heart pounding. "Let's make sure there's nothing left that ties him to us on this computer or phone."

We move quickly, erasing any trace of our presence. When we were sure our life was clean from his grasp, suddenly, my phone buzzes violently in my pocket. The screen lights up with a series of urgent texts. DOME. DOME. DOME. This alert meant something was happening bad and that we had to get down to the bottom of it.

"Y'all get that," I say.

Bambi removes her phone and nods her head. "Yeah, I got it."

Race glanced down at her phone too. "Yeah...I got...I got it too."

"Something is popping off on the streets!" Bambi yells. "We got to get the fuck out of here!"

RACE

When we made it back home the room's atmosphere was intense. Myself, Bambi and Denim were waiting on the fellas to sort shit out. No one was easy and I can feel the adrenaline pumping through my veins.

I say, my voice steady but urgent, "Did you find out anything yet, Bambi?"

Her phone dings and she looks up at all of us slowly. "The streets are saying that the coke was fake. And that Ramirez is getting questioned."

"What coke?" I ask.

"The...the coke from the package that they returned."

We all exchange a look. "That doesn't make sense!" I say.

"Hold up, where is Ramirez?" Bambi asks.

My eyes widen. "I...I don't know."

"Did he check the package before he redistributed it?"

I look down. "I mean I think so. Why else would he...I mean..." My mind spins remembering how I saw him recently. "I can't say for sure."

Bambi takes off running and I hear her yell, "Get the fellas! We at war!"

BAMBI

We gather in the boardroom, the air thick with tension. Denim, Race, Bradley, and I are all here, anxiously trying to reach Ramirez. But his phone just rings and rings, with no answer. But I'm dressed in fatigues and a white t-shirt, ready for whatever comes next.

"Where the hell is he?" Denim mutters, her frustration evident. She looks at Race. "Call him again."

"I already did. He's not answering!"

The room is filled with an uneasy silence, agitated by everyone persistently calling his phone. Each second that ticks by heightens the tension, making the air feel almost suffocating.

Suddenly Kevin bursts into the room, his expression grim. "I can't find him."

"Fuck!" I say.

"I know, baby," he kisses me and I shove him back. I still want a divorce so I don't know what he putting on a show for. "Everybody strapped?" He asks, his eyes scanning the room.

We all nod, the seriousness of the situation sinking in. The metallic click of guns being checked and loaded echoes throughout and my heart pounds in my chest, but my face remains calm.

"I have to say something," Race says.

"What is it?" I ask.

"Ramirez is on drugs."

My brows raise. "What...what are you talking about?"

"He's using."

"That's a fucking lie!" I yell.

"Nah, it's true," Bradley says.

Kevin glares. "Hold up, nigga. You knew?"

"Kevin, it's a long story," Bradley says.

"I knew too," Denim says.

"So everyone knew but me and Kevin?" I ask.

Silence.

"If what you saying is true, there's a possibility that my brother may be out there wrong."

"I think I know where he may be," Race says. "On his blocks."

The words hang heavy in the air, and I take a deep breath, feeling the weight of the moment. "You mean copping?"

She nods.

"Oh my God! He hit that hard?" I pause. "We gotta go get him. Together."

Kevin nods. "Together."

The room falls silent as we all prepare for what lies ahead. The sense of unity and purpose is strong, but so is the fear of what we might find. We've faced threats before, but this feels different.

This feels personal.

As we gear up and head out, the night air is cool, the darkness wrapping around us like a cloak.

We move quickly, our footsteps silent on the pavement on the way to our vehicles. We are in two smoked out Escalades and me, Kevin and Race were in one. Bradley and Denim were in the other. The drive to Ramirez's block is tense, the silence in the truck speaks volumes. Every shadow and street seems to hide a potential threat as we make it to the city. Kevin feels jumpy but I know why.

He is worried for me.

When I glance over, I can see that his grip on the steering wheel is tight, his knuckles white. "When we get out there stay sharp," he whispers, his eyes scanning the dark streets.

"You preaching to a soldier," I say.

As we approach Ramirez's block, the tension ratchets up another notch. The area is faintly lit, the streetlights casting long shadows on everything. We park a short distance away, our eyes fixed on the building where we hope to find Ramirez.

I get out first, my hand on my weapon. No hover. No floating above. I got my finger on the trigger of this bitch.

Kevin is at my side. Everyone else follows.

We move as one, my senses heightened. This is not only the place where he may be getting busted, but it's also the set that received the fake coke. I'm not sure, but I have a feeling someone knew he had a habit and led him out here with the promise of drugs, to bring us to the block.

Well guess what, here we are.

The sound of our breathing is loud in the otherwise silent night. The block is filled with the usual sights of decay, but tonight it feels more menacing. We're on guard when suddenly we spot him. Ramirez is slumped against a wall, his eyes glazed over. My heart lurches forward when I see my brother-in-law in this condition. Seeing him like this, so vulnerable and lost, agitates my anger. Anger at him and whatever reasoning brought him here.

Who has it all and falls this hard?

Bradley and Denim aim in the background, because we don't know who may be out there on some set up shit. But not everyone is so cautious.

"Fuck that shit!" Race pushes forward and she is the first to reach him, her voice trembling. She tucks her weapon on her hip and lowers down. "Ramirez, what the fuck you doing out here?"

He looks up, his eyes unfocused. "I'm sorry," he slurs, his voice barely audible. "They...they told me to come because—."

"Because what?" I ask. "You out here fucked up when we got business that needs cleaned up. I mean, you didn't check the shipment before you gave it back?"

"Bambi, maybe he can't answer right now," Kevin says. "Let's get him in the truck and—."

"Fuck that! We gotta know now."

Ramirez drags a hand down his face. "She's right. It was...it was on me. I checked the upper bricks. And they…they were legit. I didn't…I didn't have time to check the others on the bottom though. Since the top bricks were right I assumed they all were." I'm sorry. I…I didn't know."

Kevin steps forward. "Why you out here like this?"

"It doesn't matter," I say. "We got the answer we needed. So let's get him home. Now."

As Bradley and Kevin lift Ramirez, he mumbles incoherently, his body limp and uncooperative. He was just talking but now appears in and out. The journey back to the trucks feels like eternity, every second filled with fear.

Protecting each other fully, we finally reach the trucks, and I take one last look around, my senses on high alert.

"There them niggas go right there!" A woman yells.

Kevin peered and we all saw a pregnant woman. "I knew you should've killed that bitch!" Bradley says.

I'm confused but it doesn't matter. Because that's when the first bullet made its way to us. That one shot opened Ramirez's skull like a watermelon, and we all were covered in his blood.

"Fuck!" Kevin screamed. "They got Ram!"

"They killed my fucking brother!" Bradley yells.

Race was stuck looking at his body until I nudged her to the present.

They dropped him and fired in the direction of the bullets. We all opened up and didn't let up unless it was to reload. I saw the nigga who shot him too. He was wearing a red hoodie and since I had dealings with him before, I knew his face.

"You saw that nigga?!" Race says with tears running down her cheeks as we continue to fire.

"I saw his ass!"

When the bullets slowed down, bodies were lying everywhere. Yeah it was on us that they had fake coke. But none of that mattered anymore. They spilled Kennedy blood and they had to pay.

Gun still in hand, Kevin walks up to me, kisses my forehead which I'm sure is covered with blood. I know I said kissing me earlier was the wrong time, now he's good.

He tucks his gun in his waist, I tuck mine too.

For a second we all look down at Ramirez. He doesn't even look like himself. Bradley and Kevin pace while looking up at the sky for answers. Me and Denim grab Race and don't let go. We are out there longer than we should be until eventually Kevin says, "Let's pick him up and put him in the truck."

When Ramirez's body is secured, we all pile in one ride and drive off.

With murder on our minds.

CHAPTER TWENTY-SIX
BAMBI

Why did she open the door?

A death wish?

Whatever the reason it was dumb.

Once inside we move with calculated precision as we enter Alicia Stone's house. The scent of fried food fills the air, and when I glance down at her table I see that Alicia and her brother, Lopez, had been eating fries and hot dogs.

Oh, so the plan was to look like they had been here all the time instead of airing us out on the block. There was one flaw though. They looked guilty as a mothafucka.

I'm the first to step deeper inside, followed closely by Race and Kevin. Our presence immediately shifts the atmosphere and Alicia looks confused.

"Where's your other brother?" I ask, my voice steady but cold. "Glacey?"

Alicia's eyes dart around nervously. "He's...he's in the bathroom."

We move through the small house with purpose. The sounds of our footsteps blend with the creaking floorboards. Finally, we reach the bathroom door and I bang on it hard with the barrel of my gun.

"Glacey, come out. Now."

Silence.

"If you don't open, we firing it up. Either way we getting in."

There's a moment of silence but finally the door creaks open and he steps out, cowering in his navy-blue boxers, his eyes wide with terror. The sight of him disgusts me, but I keep my composure.

"Where the fuck is that hoodie, nigga?" Kevin asks.

"The red one," I say.

"In the bathroom."

"Good, because you gonna be buried in it." I pause. "Despite killing my brother-in-law, I already know it wasn't your order," I say calmly. "So who was behind it?"

He looks confused. "Huh?"

"Whose behind the stolen package? And the package returning? Even tonight's shoot out! Because I know it doesn't take that long to realize the coke was off. That meant y'all waited until now to use this against us. So who was behind it?" I ask, stepping closer. "Talk, nigga," Kevin says.

Glacey's eyes flick to Alicia. "Will my sister be okay? After all of this?"

Kevin moves closer, his voice menacing. "Depends. On what you say."

He swallows hard. "It was Ovay. He's been skimming off the top for a while. Ramirez knew about it and was sworn to secrecy after they found out he was using."

"You lying, nigga!" Bradley says. "You really want us to believe my brother would steal from us?"

"It's true." The words hit us hard. "Ovay was behind this. Like I said, he was gonna push off years ago on y'all from a past beef but waited until the time was right."

Race looks at us. "We caught Ovay stealing eight years back and cut him off. I thought the nigga moved out of town or somebody hit him. Didn't know he was still on the brick."

"Nah...he was alive. He was getting so much money from Ramirez letting him steal to keep his secret that he let it go," Glacey continued. "But the other day Ramirez told him y'all were getting out the game cause of that county shit y'all bought, which meant no more money. So he wanted to hurt Ramirez and ruin your rep with his people by saying y'all passing out bunk for bricks."

I step even closer, my eyes narrowing. "What about the fucking drones?"

He shakes his head frantically. "I don't know nothing about no drones."

Kevin's eyes bore into him. "Where is Ovay now?"

Glacey looks defeated. "Bambi, you hit him earlier tonight. In the head. He was next to me. He dead."

I take a deep breath. I'm glad I slayed his ass. "Are you ready?"

He nods, his face reddening. "Is there anything I can do to stay alive? I will do anything you —."

"No, nigga!" Race says holding a gun to his head. "You killed my husband it's time to die hard!"

"Wait! Wait!" He raised his hands in the air. "Can we do it in the bedroom? So my sister won't see me?"

Race looks at Alicia who is weeping and at me. "It's up to you," I say.

She looks at Kevin and Bradley. "Do what you wanna. Just make sure his blood pours."

She looks at him. "Nah, fuck this nigga." She shoots him in the eye, and he drops at his sister's feet. Alicia faints and Lopez drops down and grabs his loopy body.

"Feel better?" I ask Race.

"No. But he ain't better either."

We move toward the door, but I turn around and shoot Alicia and Lopez in the chest. If it's fuck my family, it's fuck his too.

CHAPTER TWENTY-SEVEN
BAMBI

The kitchen is empty when I first walk inside. I take a deep breath, the weight of Ramirez's death pressing heavily on my shoulders. One by one, everyone else enters. Kevin follows me, then Race wearing shades to hide her red eyes from crying, Bradley, and finally Denim. We fucked up around here.

Bad.

When we're at the dining room table I clear my throat, breaking the silence. "So we're in agreement that Melo can't know about Ram right now. Until after this Kennedy Court situation," I say, my voice firm.

"He's gonna ask for him, bae," Kevin says. "He made clear he wants all of us there."

"We gotta keep it quiet because he can't even have an open casket funeral. That shit looks like a gang hit, which is what he doesn't want. So can we agree?"

They all nod.

"On the way over here, I thought about something. After tonight, I realize we've been thinking about the drone shit in all the wrong ways," I continue. "We may have three separate issues. The detective was about to push off and we caught him so for now that situation is resolved."

"Detective?" Kevin asks.

"I'll explain that to all of you later," I say, looking at Denim who looks away. "But he hadn't made any moves yet. Second, there's the supply that was taken and returned. We know who was behind that now. But I think the drones shit is a separate situation. That's why everyone we ask about it seems to be confused."

Race shakes her head, her expression hidden behind her shades. "Now is not the time," she says abruptly.

"I'm sorry, sis. I just want to get ahead of all this because we're still under threat."

"Well why you doing this extra shit please remember that my fucking husband's head was just blown the fuck off! So maybe we can pause for one fucking second! Please!" Race leaves the room quickly and I follow close behind.

RACE

I sit on the edge of my bed, the weight of everything that has happened pressing down on me. Ramirez and I used to beef all the time, but he was still my person. My husband, even when we fought. Don't get me going about the guilt I feel from pushing him away.

I thought we had more time to make it right.

I was wrong.

My face is pressed into the pillow when the door creaks open, and Bambi steps inside. "I'm sorry about the way I left," I say.

"That was me," she says softly. "I didn't consider your feelings."

I look up at her, the pain still fresh. "Probably because you and Kevin been on good terms and me and Bradley haven't," I reply, my voice tinged with bitterness. "I didn't feel like you needed to hear any bad news."

"I asked Kevin for a divorce so shit ain't sweet with us either."

My eyes widen. "Bambi, no!"

"I can't think about that right now." She takes a seat beside me. "I know you need time to grieve. And I want to give you that. But we need to talk about what happens next."

I take a deep breath, pushing the grief down. Bambi is on her general shit with no time for pauses. I can see her military training activated.

"I know I don't have any time to think about Ramirez," I say, forcing the words out. "But I was hoping for at least tonight."

It seems like forever. She moves around and shifts a little before finally saying, "Okay. I can give you tonight. But tomorrow you gotta pour a little out to Ramirez and be downstairs ready to take next steps." She turns to walk away.

"Bambi, has your opinion changed about Scarlett? I know last time you said no. Do you still believe the drone shit ain't her? It's the last open question."

She turns back around. "I believe the drones involves her, but I don't know how. The problem I'm having is that I'm trying to figure out her motive. If it was her, and she has our address, why hasn't she made a move?"

"I have something to show you."

CHAPTER TWENTY-EIGHT
BAMBI

M elo comes home, and the whole house feels like we died. To make matters worse, we have to fake happy so he doesn't know that his uncle was murdered. The sun streams through the windows, casting a warm glow over everything, but we're not in the mood to celebrate. Not to mention the stranger in our house...the tailor who is ready and waiting to make him look like a star for the Kennedy Court celebration.

When we see his car drive up, Kevin and I exchange a tense look. He grabs my hands.

"We're only doing this for Melo, Kevin. I'm serious about wanting a divorce."

"And I'm serious about you staying in my life."

I hear a car door close, and I tug him. "Let's fake the excitement for Melo. We'll get into everything else later."

"Agreed. But just so you know, I'm not letting my wife go."

When Melo walks through the door, he grabs me in a strong hug, lifting me off my feet. When he's done with me,

Kevin gives him the type of embrace that only a father could.

"It's so good to see both of you," he says smiling with his entire being.

"It's good to have you home," I say.

He looks harder at me. "Ma, are you sure you're okay?"

"Of...of course I am, baby!"

"What I want to know is, are you ready?" Kevin says, saving me from his scrutiny. That's what you call teamwork. "Because the tailor's been waiting on you for hours! It's time to get fit, Rockefeller!"

Kevin leads him to the tailor, who begins the work on his suit in the living room, pins and fabric swatches scattered around. As we engage in simple convo, Kevin and I are careful with our mannerisms for fear Melo will pick up on something being wrong. That meant every time he looked over at us, we had to fake a smile. And when you feel grief like we do, that's the hardest fucking thing in the world.

Still, standing in front of me, tall and glowing with brown skin and a chiseled body like his father at his age, I feel like if nothing else happened, I did something right.

"Look at you, all grown up," Kevin says, pride evident in his voice. He adjusts the lapel of Melo's suit jacket, a smile stretching across his face.

I nod, beaming. "We're so proud, Melo. This is a big move for you."

He walks up to me and grabs the top of my arms. Looking into my eyes, he says, "Again, it's a big move for us. This is for all of us. My uncles too."

"Your mother knows," Kevin says.

Why the fuck do I keep forgetting the lie? Maybe because my unconscious knows I never want out of the game.

"Where is uncle Bradley and Uncle Ramirez? And aunt Denim and aunt Race?"

My stomach drops, and I try to hide the fact that Ramirez is murdered. Luckily, a few moments later, the doorbell rings. "What's that?" I ask.

"The surprise." Melo heads to answer it, and Kevin and I exchange a look of excitement. When he returns, he's not alone. A woman is with him, and she looks stunning in a sleek but classy black dress that hugs her curves. Her pink hair lights up the room, and her presence immediately adds a spark of energy to the space.

"Mom, Dad, this is Electra," Melo says, his voice filled with pride. "My lady."

Electra smiles warmly, extending her hand. Immediately, I don't like her. But why?

"It's a pleasure to meet you both," she says.

Kevin and I shake her hand, our smiles plastered like statues. "The pleasure is ours," I say. "Welcome to our home."

Electra blushes slightly, then excuses herself to the bathroom, clearly needing a moment to compose herself. It's like she couldn't handle the weight of my stare.

Melo watches her go, then turns back to us, a secretive grin on his lips. "What is it, son?"

"I've got something to tell you both."

Kevin and I lean in, our curiosity piqued. "We're listening" Kevin says.

Melo takes a deep breath, his smile widening. "I'm going to propose to her at the Kennedy Court opening. In front of the press and everything!"

The words hang in the air for a moment. If my instincts are right, he won't be marrying her because her energy makes me sick to my stomach. And I intend on finding out why. Instead, I smile. "That's great, Melo."

He leans closer. "You sure you feel that way, Ma? Because you look off."

I grin. "Of course I do."

Kevin gives him a handshake before pulling him closer. "Congratulations, son! We're pulling out all the stops for this celebration too! It's going to be perfect."

When Melo returns to the tailor, I rush outside.

CHAPTER TWENTY-NINE
MELO

*M*elo stands in his room, watching his fiancée, Electra, as she explores his space. The room is filled with photos and personal items from his younger years...posters of his favorite bands, sports trophies, and photos with his family.

"This place is huge. I can't believe you really grew up like this."

"We actually lived somewhere else, but they moved my stuff here. When my twin was alive shit was good. But — ."

"You had a twin?"

"Yes. But it's a long story."

"How come you never told me that before?"

"When we first met that night...so much went down. Like...I lost time and then when I woke up you were in my bed. I had some wild ass thoughts of things I thought happened. Even ideas of my brother telling me to run."

"So your twin brother who is no longer alive doesn't like me?"

"Not saying that. Anyway it was years ago. I just...after that night when we continued to get to know one another, I just figured I would tell you when the time was right. Just never got right until now."

Electra nods. It was a sensitive topic she could tell. And without getting into too much detail she figured Bambi was the cause. Looking at a photo of Melo and his twin brother, both grinning widely she says, "What was it like being in this family?"

"You mean being rich?"

She grins.

Melo sighs, leaning against the doorframe. "It was great, but I always felt like I needed to do more, to be more. That's why I moved to Houston. I needed to prove to myself that I could make something of my own. And that's how the Kennedy Court Development was born and of course how I met you."

Electra turns to him, a soft smile on her lips. He had no idea that she did not live in Houston like he believed. Melo was clueless on the plan Scarlett had laid because he moved to get away from such traps. He failed.

"I like that. It shows you're driven, that you care about building something meaningful."

Melo's smile widens. "Yeah, it's been a dream of mine for a long time. I wanted to create something that would make my family proud, something that would last."

She walks over to him and places a hand on his cheek. "You've done an amazing job, Melo. They're proud of you." She kisses his lips. "And I'm proud of you too."

He leans into her touch, feeling a sense of contentment wash over him. "Thanks, Electra. It means a lot to hear you say that."

Electra steps back, glancing around the room one last time. "I have to go to the bathroom. Be right back."

"You can use the one in my room."

"Nah, I get nervous. Don't want you to see me like that."

He chuckles. "There is one down the hall to the right."

As she leaves the room, a subtle shift in her expression is apparent. There is a sinister energy about her that Melo remains blissfully unaware of.

Something is about to pop off.

Electra leaves Melo's room and walks down the hallway, her footsteps barely making a sound. Just like a snake, she slithers quietly. Undetected. Unseen. At the moment, the house is filled with the quiet hum of family life, but her mind is focused on a different mission.

After much snooping, she approaches another room and gently opens the door. Inside, Master is sitting at his desk, focused on a book. He looks up, surprised to see her.

"Hello," Electra says, her voice smooth and friendly. "I'm a friend of your mommy."

Master's eyes widen slightly. "Denim?"

Electra shakes her head, a small smile playing on her lips. "No, your real mother. Scarlett. She wants to meet you."

Suddenly his confusion turns to curiosity. "My real mother. She wants to meet me? Is that the one who my uncle sends the videos to?"

Electra nods, stepping further into the room. "Yes. Do you want that?"

Master hesitates for a moment, then nods. "Yes, I want to meet her. When can I do it?"

"I'll work on that." Her smile broadens. "But I appreciate you telling me yes, because that makes things easier." She pats him on the head and talks to him a bit longer, before leaving the room.

Electra continues down the hallway, her mind set on the next step of her plan. Before long, she finds Bambi sitting in the dimly lit living room, a serene look on her face. The soft glow from the lamps emits long shadows on the walls, adding an air of mystery to the room.

"Mind if I join you for a drink?" Electra asks, her tone casual.

Bambi looks up and nods. Getting an opportunity to size the sneak up was not something on her bingo card. And yet here she was.

"Sure, have a seat." She pours a glass of wine for Electra, and they clink their glasses together before she takes a seat.

"Cheers," Electra says, taking a sip. "You're such a good mother."

"That's a curious statement from someone who has no idea who I am. But why do you say that?"

"Melo told me so much about his childhood. How you always made the best meals and how you always had a good time with them. His twin too. It's so important that a mother takes care of her son. Don't you agree?"

Bambi crosses her legs. "That's the realest shit you said all day."

She takes another sip. "So tell me, what happened to your other son? The twin?"

Bambi frowns. "I'm not going to get into that. I choose to focus on our good times. What I do remember is how he and his brother were always running around, causing trouble. But they had good hearts." She takes a sip. "What I wouldn't give to see them growing up together."

Electra nods and whips her pink hair over her shoulder.

Bambi drinks everything in her glass and pours another. "You like your hair, don't you? I can tell by how much you play in it."

"Hair is the antennas to a woman's soul."

"Is that right?" Bambi winks. "I'll remember that."

"Melo mentioned how you used to read them stories before bed and how they'd always beg for one more chapter."

Bambi chuckles. "Those were the days. Melo was always so curious, always asking questions."

The room falls into a comfortable silence, filled only with the sound of their glasses touching the table and the distant hum of the house. Then, Electra's energy shifts and her smile fades. "Speaking of questions, Bambi, I have one for you."

"I'm listening."

"How well do you know your friends? Race Kennedy."

Bambi's smile falters. "What you mean?"

Electra reaches into her bag and pulls out her phone. She shows Bambi a video of Race assaulting a man in public. Shocked, Bambi rises from her seat. "Where the fuck did you get this?" Bambi demands.

She tucks it into the pocket of her dress. "Does that really matter? Or do you really want to know what I will do with it?"

"Bitch, don't play with me!"

Electra smirks. "This is just the beginning. If you don't return Master to Scarlett, I'll ruin Melo's life. Your only living son. And if you tell him about any of this, and he confronts me, I will show the video to the world. I'm sure they will be interested in the man whose family are drug dealers and whose in-laws are serial assaulters. Even while continuing to buy up property in the DMV area. Because I – ."

Her words were cut short when Bambi yanks her body to the floor by her hair and put her manicured foot on her neck. With the gun in her face she bends down and says, "Open your mouth."

She doesn't.

"OPEN YOUR FUCKING MOUTH, WHORE! Because we both know it's not your first time.

She widens her jaws and Bambi slips the gun inside of her mouth and presses on her tongue causing an immediate gag response. Bambi has done this before. "Listen to me, you going to get out of here and never return to my house. And you going to leave my son alone too. Do you understand?"

Since she couldn't talk Bambi said, "Nod if you do."

She nods.

Bambi presses down on her neck again and slowly removes the gun and her foot. "Now get the fuck out!"

Electra stands up leisurely, her smile returning. Then she walks away slyly, leaving Bambi standing in the low light.

"Just so you know, if you kill me, I do have copies."

The moment was intense. Neither knowing that Denim heard every word.

CHAPTER THIRTY
BAMBI

After checking that bitch, and locking Master in his room, I rush toward Melo's room. Because it's clear Scarlett for sure knows where we live now. Before entering I take a deep breath, trying to steady my nerves. Then I push inside.

"Melo, sweetheart, can we talk for a minute?" I ask, my voice softer than usual, masking the tension beneath.

Melo moves closer. "Sure, Mom. What's up?"

I smile, trying to keep things light. "I wanted to ask you about Electra. Where did you meet her?"

He raises an eyebrow, probably sensing something is off. "Why you want to know?"

I keep my tone casual. "Just curious. She seems like a nice girl, and I want to know more about her."

He nods. "To be honest we met in Houston years ago. Things got a little out of hand but we vibed the next day. She was my friend at first and then we got more serious."

"How did things get out of hand?"

"Ma, don't go there."

"Understood," I say, forcing a smile. "She seems very... confident."

He chuckles. "Yeah, she is. That's one of the things I love about her. She reminds me of you."

Gross as fuck, but I nod, choosing my next words carefully. "Melo, I just want to make sure you're happy. Are you sure about her? Are you sure she's the one?"

His eyes narrow slightly. "Why you asking me this now?"

I take a deep breath. "I just... have a strange feeling about her and I want to be sure she's right for you."

His expression hardens. "Mom, you don't need to worry about that. I know what I'm doing."

"I'm sure you do, but—"

"But what?" He interrupts, his voice rising. "Are you trying to mess up my life?"

I shake my head. "No, Melo. I just want to protect—."

"Protect me from what?" He snaps. "From being happy?"

I flinch at his tone. "No, from getting hurt. I've been through a lot, and I don't want you to experience the same pain by giving the Kennedy name to someone who's not worthy."

He moves even closer to me. "Mom, I love you. But I'm in love with her. And I'm going to propose. If you want to stay in my life, stay out the way. That goes for pops too."

He walks out.

I storm into Race's lab, my heart pounding. The metallic scent of machinery and the sharp tang of chemicals assault my senses, but I push forward, my eyes locked on Race. She looks up from her workbench, surprised by my sudden entrance.

"What the fuck do you do in your spare time?" I demand, my voice echoing off the sterile walls. "And don't lie to me."

Race laughs it off. "Nothing, Bambi. Why you coming at me like this? You know I gotta plan Ramirez's funeral."

"Don't lie to me!" I snap, stepping closer. "I saw the videos of you doing all kinds of wild shit. Stabbing niggas. Cutting niggas! I guess we didn't find all the tapes from that fucking detective's office. But guess who has them now? Scarlett! And she using the bitch Electra to get at me."

"Are you sure? I mean where is this coming from, Bambi?"

"I just fucking told you! What kind of weirdo shit are you into, Race?"

Race looks genuinely puzzled, shaking her head. "I don't know why I did it. Or do it. The urge just comes over me and I move on it. But I stopped since the war popped off."

I feel my heart rate accelerating even more. "What you did gave that bitch some ammunition. And it's gonna ruin everything. My relationship with Melo could be destroyed because of this. Do you fucking understand? I mean this whore literally has videos."

"What does she want?"

"Master. She wants Master!"

"Fuck it! Let her show the videos!" Race's face hardens with determination. "I'm willing to be sacrificed because I deserve that shit. I'll go to the authorities to prevent it from coming out myself."

"No the fuck you not either." I shake my head. "You still a Kennedy and I won't risk losing you. I got a feeling even if she gets what she wants, it will come out whether you turn yourself in or not. We in this together so cut all that extra shit out. And the crazy shit you do on the streets too!"

Race steps closer, her eyes pleading. "But I don't want you to give up Master, Bambi. Don't let them win."

I clench my fists. "That ain't the worst part. I believe she has something else on us. I mean the way that smug face bitch looked at me proves it." I punch the air.

Race glares, her energy mirroring mine. "Well I gave you the info you needed earlier. So let's move on what we discussed. You were right that we are under threat and that there is no use in waiting."

Suddenly, Denim walks in and I shake my head. "Denim, we talking now. Can you come back in—."

"You tried to lie about not having secrets, and now it's all come out," she says to Race.

"Wait, how did you hear?" Bambi asks.

"It doesn't matter."

Race sighs. "I know, Denim. I messed up. I just... I guess I was too embarrassed to let anybody in on that shit."

Denim glares harder. "The wild part is I read about you in the fucking paper and had no idea it was you. Messed my mind up about all the violent ass shit you were doing out there!"

"It wasn't just Race with secrets," I say, looking between them. "So if she's to blame I am too."

"Both of y'all...damn." Denim says before shaking her head. "What I find fucked up is that I came clean the other day and both of you lied! What kind of shit is that?"

"My situation is boring," I admit. "I been dealing with someone on the low. He visits me in the apartment."

Denim looks at her, surprised. "What? Who?"

"A guy named Lucas. And we been seeing each other when the mood hits but it's nothing more than that."

"Why you coming clean now?"

"Because whether you do shit as wild as what Race got going on, or as whorish as me, it still don't change the fact that we gotta stick together."

"She's right." Race looks at me and then at Denim. "No more secrets."

"No more secrets," I say.

Denim looks between us, then nods slowly. "Okay. No more secrets."

We all hug, a sense of relief that we are locked back in.

"Now let's make our next move!" I say.

CHAPTER THIRTY-ONE
BAMBI

I t's time!

I sit in the car with Race, the tension thick. Kevin and Bradley are in the back, their silence mirroring the heaviness in the air. While Denim is at home with Master, keeping him safe.

With my mind still spinning, I turn to Race while she's driving, needing more answers. "Tell me again how the face recognition thing you use works."

Race glances at me, then looks back at the road. "It's no different than any other face recognition service. Except it's underground. You take a picture of a person's face, and you'll find the address, where they work, social media sites and everything. Within seconds. As long as they take one picture at home, this app will know their location."

I take a deep breath.

Kevin says, "Why didn't you tell her before if you had the address?"

Race's hands grip the steering wheel tighter, and I can see the fear in her eyes. "Bambi...I was gonna—"

I cut her off, my voice sharp. "Answer the question."

She hesitates, then finally speaks. "I found out once I snapped her recent photo at the park. That led me to two locations. One of them I went to without even telling you. Like…I guess I wanted to do the leg work first. That way if I needed to present her address, it would be accurate. It was an old apartment building so nothing materialized. The second address I haven't been to yet."

"Why so late to say something, Race?" Bradley asks. "Still waiting on an answer!"

Race sighs. "Because I felt bad for what I did to Scarlett. I believe I was the reason why she didn't have a relationship with her son. The guilt weighed down on me ever since I had her jumped." She looks at me. "And I was about to give Bambi the information, but I wanted to know if you thought she was involved with the drones first, when you saw her in the parking lot with Bradley."

I stare at her, my anger simmering. "And?"

"When you said you believed she wasn't, I decided against it. But now, I realize she's not after sending Electra. That she's a threat. So she's a threat to all of us."

"But we were putting trackers on her car for nothing. You had everything we needed to know." I don't bring up that she was using the app to hurt men in front of the fellas.

I'll keep her secret and hope Denim does the same. But Race was wrong for this.

Kevin and Bradley exchange looks in the backseat as we head to this whore's house.

We hired six men to crawl all over Scarlett's house. As big as it is I can tell she came into money. Definitely enough dough to order drones.

Dressed in all black, Kevin, Race, Bradley, and I wait in the car, ready for everything as they silently slip through the shadows towards her crib. It's mostly dark, the only light coming from the lights on the property.

From our position, we watch as the men skillfully pick the lock and open the front door gaining easy entry before disarming the alarm. Scarlett must not be home.

With a silent signal, they flood the residence, disappearing into the shadows. I grip the handle of the car door, ready to move at any moment.

Minutes pass, feeling like hours, before we get the all-clear. We move swiftly, entering the house behind our hired men. It's definitely Scarlett's home. The familiar scent of her favorite perfume lingers in the air, mingling with the aroma of fresh spaghetti. A pot is still warm on the stove, a clear sign we just missed her or somebody else.

I motion for the others to continue the search while I head towards the back. I happen toward an office. The door creaks further open, revealing a cluttered desk and a shelf lined with various trinkets. My eyes immediately lock onto a blue bunny sitting on the desk.

"Why does she still have this shit if it doesn't mean anything?" I pick up the paint riddled, shot and torn up bunny. This gnarled, stitched up bitch coming with me.

Kevin joins me, his eyes narrowing at the sight of the bunny. "So *she* has it?"

"You that pressed that you still want this thing?"

"Just asking. Don't want it no more now."

I take the bunny, feeling its soft fur under my fingers. It's a chilling reminder of the games Scarlett is playing. I'm not leaving it here. She won't use it against us, I don't care if it is useless.

We continue searching the office, opening drawers and rifling through papers. I put many of them in my pockets before putting things back in regular order. While Bradley finds a phone hidden under a pile of documents.

I on the other hand go to her fridge. I don't know why I do, but when I do I see a familiar sight, so I grab it. It's a red drink.

"You thirsty?" He asks.

"Nah."

He shrugs. "Anyway, these might be useful too," he says, handing a bunch of other items to me.

When we get all we can carry I say, "Let's go. We've got what we need."

As we make our way back to the truck, I think I see a blue mustang in the distance, but I can't be sure. So I wait until it pulls off and we get into our ride.

CHAPTER THIRTY-TWO
DENIM

I'm sitting with Master in the living room, the soft hum of the television in the background. I hope my family gets the answers they need tonight. So we can protect the fort. And I hope that everything comes back together, including the bond with my husband.

The house is quiet, a rare moment of peace amidst the chaos. All of a sudden, Master looks up at me, his big brown eyes filled with curiosity.

"Mommy, can I ask you something?" He says, his voice small and hesitant.

"Of course, sweetie. What's on your mind?" I reply, brushing a strand of hair from his forehead.

"Can I see my real mother?" His question hits me like a punch to the gut.

I pause, trying to keep my voice steady. "Where did you get that idea from, baby?" Electra's bitch ass must've touched the boy before she got to Bambi.

Damn!

We slipping!

He fidgets with the hem of his shirt. "The lady with pink hair told me I could see her. She said my real mother wants to see me too."

I feel a surge of anger and fear. "Master, we your real family. I'm your mommy now, and we all love you very much. So it's best to leave it alone, okay?"

"But I want to know her," he insists, his eyes pleading.

I take a deep breath, trying to hide my frustration. "I understand, but sometimes it's better not to dig up the past. Like I said, we're your family, and that's what matters now."

He looks down, clearly upset and not feeling the Kennedy brand one bit. "Okay," he mutters. "Can I go outside to Uncle Ramirez's cave and play paintball?"

"No, Master." I say feeling sad again that Ram is gone.

Master pouts, and then, his mood shifts. "I'm hungry."

I smile, trying to lighten the mood. Because if there was one thing I could do, feeding his ass was it. "How about I make you a sandwich? Your favorite."

He nods, his face brightening a little. "Yes, please!"

I head to the kitchen, trying to shake off the unease that Electra's meddling stirred up in our home. Too much happening too quick! It's hard to keep up. Once propped up, I make Master his favorite sandwich, peanut butter and jelly before cutting the crusts off just like he likes it. When I return to the living room, my heart stops.

Master is gone.

I place the plate down on the floor. I don't know why but him being gone scared me and panic sets in as I search the house, calling his name. They always say I can't be trusted and here I go. Losing him at a time like this!

"Master! Master! Where are you? Don't fucking play with me!" I sound like a slave. "Master!"

No response.

I check every room, my anxiety growing with each passing second. My mind races with possibilities, each one more terrifying than the last.

Did Scarlett grab him that quick?

Finally, I run to the front door, flinging it open and rushing outside. "Master!" I shout, my voice breaking.

There's no sign of him and I feel a cold dread settle in my stomach. How could this happen? I promised to protect him, to keep him safe. Bambi gonna fuck me up behind this shit.

I grab my phone and frantically dial her number to get the shit over with, my hands shaking. "Bambi, it's Master! He's gone!"

"Fuck you mean he gone?!"

"I'm sorry! I don't know what happened!"

"Stay there! I'm in route!"

CHAPTER THIRTY-THREE
MELO

*M*elo sways gently with Electra in his arms, the soft music filling the luxurious hotel suite. The chandelier above emits a warm, golden glow. The world outside their embrace seems to fade away, leaving just the two of them in their own intimate bubble.

Electra looks up at him, her eyes shimmering. "Your mother doesn't like me," she says softly, her voice carrying a hint of sadness.

Melo frowns slightly, not wanting to believe it but knowing deep down that his mother has her reservations. Besides, she told him straight up. "I don't think that's true. She just needs time to get to know you. Like I do."

"Unless she got a dick and it's in my mouth, I doubt she'll ever see my true potential."

"Cut it out."

Electra's expression turns more serious. "You know how your mother is, Melo. She has her own ways, her own rules. I just want to know where you stand. If it came down to smoke, who would you pick?"

His heart skips a beat at the question. "Please, don't try and make me choose between you and my family. It won't end well because I don't like ultimatums."

She sighs, resting her head against his chest. "After the stories you told me eight or so years ago, you alone know the things your mother is capable of. If I have a chance to take you away from all that, where is the problem?"

Melo pulls back slightly, looking into her eyes. The weight of her words hangs heavy between them. "I just... I need a minute to think."

"You mean right now?"

"What better time?"

She kisses his lips and steps away. The moment her face is out of view, she glares.

BAMBI

The vehicles were parked, and we were rushing toward our house when my phone rings. Bradley and Race are already inside, probably to look for Master, leaving me and Kevin alone.

My phone continued to ring. I glance at the screen and see Melo's name.

"You good, Bambi?" Kevin asks touching my arm.

"It's our son." I take a deep breath and answer, my voice shaking slightly. "Melo, is everything okay, honey?"

"Mom, I'm sorry for how I talked to you earlier. I just... I want us to be better than this," he says, his tone filled with regret.

I close my eyes, the pain in his voice cutting deep. "I know, baby. We'll get through this."

"Just so you know I pushed the Kennedy Court unveiling back a few days."

I was relieved but surprised. "Really? Why?"

"Because uncle Ramirez missing in action, and I want us all there. So it gives us more time to come together." He exhales. "Where's dad?"

"Right here. But before I give him the phone, where are you, son?"

"Don't worry about me. I'm fine," he says.

"Melo, you gotta be safe right now. Even if you around people you love."

"Like you?" He says.

"Like every fucking body."

I hand the phone to Kevin, who takes it with a solemn nod. As he speaks to Melo, I notice a single drone hovering overhead. My heart skips a beat, but I keep my composure, not wanting to alarm anyone.

Kevin finishes his call and hands the phone back to me. "He's gone."

"Kevin, look in the sky."

"What the fuck is that?"

"Another drone!" I yell.

I take a deep breath, my mind racing. I have a sinking feeling I know what's happening, but I need to be sure. You can't get to our property through driving because you couldn't make it through the many gates. But the air...you got us there.

"Let's get out of here," I say, my voice firm. "We need to find Master."

CHAPTER THIRTY-FOUR
BAMBI

Me and Bradley were sitting in the living room to operate the next part of my plan. With Electra having her claws in Melo and Master going missing the house was in an uproar. But I was focused knowing exactly what to do next.

"Bradley, remember what we talked about. When you call her, be calm. Everything from this moment on is strategic. Because I see the end goal in my mind clear as fuck!"

"This better bring my nephew back."

"If I'm right, it will."

Bradley nods, pulling out his phone and dialing her number. He has to call five times before she finally picks up.

"What the fuck do you want?"

I snatch the phone on account of him moving too slow. I know Master is their blood nephew, but they don't care like me for real for real. I'm a mother. There's a difference. "Scarlett, it's me! Don't hang up!"

"What do you want, bitch?!"

"Do you have Master?" I begin, cutting straight to the point.

"So you lost my son?"

"Don't play with me!" I yell. "Do you have him or not?"

"Since as long as you've known me, you've played games instead of me, you have a nerve! And now you got my son wrapped up? Nah, bitch, let's do it like this, you have less than 24 hours to present him or —."

"Or what?"

"The first video with Race will go out to the world. And then the second. Trust me, you won't like what else I got in the chamber."

"What video with Race?" Bradley whispered.

I hate that she said that shit out loud and wave him off. I just pray he doesn't press me on what she's talking about later. At the same time, I knew she was holding more. "Okay...okay let me meet you."

"So all of a sudden you know where he is?"

"Yes!"

There's a pause on the other end, and I can almost hear the gears turning in her head. "You a liar."

"I'm telling the truth. But you gotta tell me what else you have, and you have to tell Electra to get lost and stay away from my son. Then I'll let you see yours."

"How do I know I can trust you?"

"Because you don't want nobody fucking with your son and I don't want nobody fucking with mine."

"Bambi, if I do this and you playing games, shit will get bad."

"Shit already bad."

She sighs. "Okay, I'll hold off on unleashing my next video for one sight of Master in person."

I take a deep breath, considering the risks. But I know we don't have much of a choice. "Agreed. You see him, we get the information, and then you leave us alone. Understood?"

Kevin and Race reenter.

"Understood," she replies, her voice laced with suspicion. "When and where?"

"I'll let you know," I say, ending the call. I hand the phone back to Bradley, my mind already racing with details.

"We need to be careful," I say, looking at Kevin, Race, and Bradley.

Kevin shakes his head. "Bambi, what are you doing? We don't have Master."

"But I now know that she doesn't either. And I think I know who does." I walk away, pause and turn back around. "Grab that bunny. It's part of all this shit."

CHAPTER THIRTY-FIVE
BAMBI

We were outside at a park.

Kevin, Bradley and Denim were with me but not near. Kevin is hidden to the right with a gun trained and ready, while Bradley is hidden in trees to the left. Denim remains in the car. And Race is in a separate vehicle, not too far away with her eyes trained on us and the surroundings. She has the bunny.

I stand alone.

Scarlett approaches. "Where is Master?"

"What else do you have, Scarlett?"

"Oh my God! I knew I couldn't trust you! You don't have my son! Once again all this was a lie!" She's trembling and if I didn't before, I definitely believe she is not involved in his disappearance now. She looks like she's about to unravel.

"What else do you have on us, Scarlett?" I look away and then back at her. "Or are you fucking lying about the other video?"

"Bambi, I want my son!" She places her hands on her mouth repeatedly and drops them. "Please...please bring him to me."

"I asked you a fucking question. What else do you have?!"

She doesn't respond. Instead she pulls out her phone and I shake my head preventing Kevin and Bradley from lighting her up. I think they thought she was taking out a gun.

When my phone dings, I realize she sent something. I glance at it quickly, keeping my expression neutral. It's a video...and it's also the worst thing I've ever seen in my life. Runs miles around the video that detective got on Race.

"Where...where did you get this from?" I move closer, one hand on my stomach. "Where...where did you get this?" I yell.

"When we lived together, before we were going to meet with the Russians. I was at her house a few times when she was blackmailing me. I found the tapes and kept them ever since," she replies, a hint of power in her voice. "You will give me my son and give me custody, or I will ruin yours and Melo's life with this video. I mean can you imagine the shame?" She says, her voice icy and resolute. "I once loved you. Don't make me burn y'all niggas down." She storms off and I do too.

When we are all inside the car I look over at Denim and then in the back at Kevin. My anger bubbling over.

"What was on the video?" He asks.

"Don't worry, my nigga. I'm gonna tell you later."

CHAPTER THIRTY-SIX
RACE

I sit in my car, the blue bunny in my lap. My fingers trace the worn fabric, and a sense of unease settles over me. There's something about this toy that doesn't sit right, and Bambi knows its secrets yet for now, she holds back.

When everyone pulls off, I analyze the photos I took earlier at the meet with Scarlett. They were pictures of her, the surroundings and the entire scene.

When my eyes catch sight of a familiar car outside. A blue 1977 Mustang, I zoom in and take a screenshot of the driver's face. A white woman with light red hair is on my screen.

"There you go. But who the hell are you?" I say, pulling up the image on my phone.

I run it through my app and facial recognition kicks in. Within seconds a name pops up and my confusion deepens because I don't recognize this person. Why is she watching us?

I hit Bambi's number from my cell. "Bambi, you there?"

"Yeah, what's up?" She answers, tension evident in her voice. "Did you find anything from when I met Scarlett?"

"I just spotted the same blue Mustang outside when we were at her house. Took a screenshot of the driver. Any idea who this is?" I send her the image.

There's a pause before Bambi responds. "The bunny is connected to the car and if I'm right, the drones."

"Yep, I believe the car is following a tracker in this stuffed animal. And I'm sure a camera is in its eyes." I hold it up and glare and I feel like someone is watching me. "We should've looked more into the eyes."

"Put me on speaker. Next to it."

I nod and do it.

"Listen, I'm not sure," Bambi says. "But if I think you are who I believe you are, your beef is not with us. If you want to talk, text me a picture of our nephew. I need to know he's alive and well. Then maybe we can work together."

When she finishes, I say, "Where you going now?"

"I got to talk to Kevin about that video. I'll see you in a few."

CHAPTER THIRTY-SEVEN
BAMBI

The weight of the world rests on my shoulders as I walk into Kevin's office. I can't get a hold of Melo and she still hasn't sent the picture of Master. But first I have to deal with this nigga over the video Scarlett sent me. It was some insidious shit.

He looks up, concern etched on his face. I'm sure he knows something's wrong, but he doesn't know the full extent of it.

"Kevin," I say, closing the door behind me. The seriousness in my voice makes him sit up straighter. "Are you that fucking gross, nigga?"

"What's going on, Bambi?" He asks standing up.

I take a deep breath, bracing myself for what I'm about to say. "Scarlett has a video. A video of you fucking…you fucking your own aunt!"

His face reddens, and he looks like he's been punched in the gut. "What…what video? When?"

"Years ago, nigga! It's obvious the bitch is bones now! Anyway it doesn't matter! If that gross shit gets out…if that horrible shit comes to light, it will tear our son apart. How could you do this to us?" My voice breaks, and I fight back the tears. "To our family!"

Kevin's eyes fill with tears, and he buries his face in his hands. "I'm so sorry, Bambi. I didn't know she was videotaping that shit."

"It doesn't matter that you didn't know! It's that you...that you fucking allowed yourself to be...to be..." The words wouldn't leave. "This is the worst kind of shit to be associated with."

He walks up to me, and I hit his hands away. He looks down. "I know you don't want to hear it but I...I...was so confused during that period in my life."

"Do you love her? Is that why you held onto the bunny and all that dumb shit?"

"No...it's just that, molestation when it happens by the hands of a woman is harder to deal with and assess. Because you need a mother figure and—."

"Nigga, I don't want to hear no public service—."

"Listen to me!" He grabs me. "This woman started with me when I didn't have anybody. No mother or any other female figure. And so she fucked with my mind." He lets me go. "I have to get help and I'm so sorry, baby. I would never want to hurt you or our family."

I sit down across from his desk, and he grabs his chair and sits in front of me. "What's your plan? Anything you decide I'm with."

I take a deep breath. "I don't know...I'm...my head is fucked up with images of what...of what she showed me."

He grabs my hand and shakes me. "Then use it! Use that energy to get revenge. If you want to hate me afterward, we can do that later. And I'll take whatever consequence that comes my way, including a divorce."

I nod. "Okay...okay...even if we get Master back —."

"When we get my nephew back."

"When that happens even if we give her custody, this will always hang over our heads. I feel it in my heart that Scarlett will never let us forget it. She wants us to have scars like she does. So, we have to go to the next level."

Kevin looks up, confusion and desperation in his eyes. "What do you know?"

I look at him, wanting so much to let him in on everything I learned about the bunny. But trust with us is ruined. "The less you know the better. Just...just let me work shit out."

When my phone vibrates and I look down, I see exactly what I've been waiting on. My nephew smiling and alive.

I show him the screen.

"Wow! The shit you be doing really do be working," He says sitting back. "I'll never doubt you again."

"And I'ma hold you to it."

CHAPTER THIRTY-EIGHT
BAMBI

The weatherman called it a tornado watch but it was cold as fuck too.

The rain pours down, drumming relentlessly on the roof of my truck. Denim and Race drive in separate vehicles per my plan, but we park side by side so we can talk to each other at the gas station. Each of us have a chore.

The wipers move back and forth, trying to keep the windshield clear, but the downpour is relentless. It's a fitting backdrop for the storm brewing inside. We're all on edge. Race is sharp and alert while Denim's fingers tap nervously on her steering wheel.

But I have to take the lead, so I take a deep breath and step out of the truck, the rain instantly soaking through my clothes.

"I'll be back," I yell. "If either of you see something not planned, honk three times. I'll hear you."

I head inside the gas station, the bell above the door chiming as I enter. The owner looks up, a bored expression on his face. Making myself known, his eyes show he recognizes me. Again, because I planned everything, I walk over to him, slipping him a wad of cash as discussed. "I'm going out back."

"I already got you. Let me know if you need anything else."

He nods, pocketing the money without another word. I exit through the back door, the rain hitting my face like tiny needles. Once back outside, I move stealthily to the side of the building, my military training kicking in. The rain is beating me up as I blend into the shadows, making my way to the blue Mustang parked just out of sight.

When ready, I take a deep breath and approach the car, my heart pounding. As I open the passenger door, which was unlocked, the woman next to me turns, her face partially hidden in the shadows.

Whoa.

For a moment I'm shook. She looks so much like someone I know its sick. When I turn my head, I'm relieved that Master is in the back.... sleep. I breathe a sigh of relief.

"Is he okay?" I ask.

She nods.

"First, I want to say thank you for not hurting him. And I...I know who you are. But I don't understand. Why you bothering my family?"

She turns fully towards me, her eyes cold and hard. "My life has been ruined," she says simply.

I narrow my eyes. "Ruined how?"

She sighed, her gaze never wavering. "It's a long story not meant for you," she begins. "One that involves a lot of betrayal, hurt, and loss. Your family is at the center of it all. I guess our worlds clashed."

"Well you got what you needed. Now I'm going to get my nephew home safely. How were you able to get onto our property to get him?"

"I knew that he loved paintball from watching him through the bunny. So, once I saw all of you were not at home, I sent a drone with a message for playing paintball that he followed right out the gates."

"Why?"

"You know why. I knew you were smart and that would lead to us meeting right now." She takes a deep breath. "But before you do anything, look at him hard."

"Who you talking about?"

"You'll know when it's time." I absorb her words, not knowing what they meant.

"Okay, are you ready for what happens next?" I pause. "I mean really?"

"I been waiting on this moment all my life."

Satisfied with my conversation with the stranger, I retrace my steps back to the front of the station soaking wet. I have Master's hand in my own and he's barely awake. Still, I force him up and walk him over to Race's car because at this age he's too heavy to carry. "Take him home."

"Everything okay?" Race asks, her voice tense.

I nod slightly, wiping the rain from my face. "Yes, just get him home, and do what you gotta and meet us back here."

"Don't worry. I got you," Race says. "I'ma make you proud."

I look at Denim. "I need you to go to that pet store and get what I asked for."

Denim nods. "This all sounds wild but okay. Where you going?"

"I'm meeting Kevin. To see a man about a boy." I walk away.

Both of them start their cars and peel out.

CHAPTER THIRTY-NINE
ZAYDEN

Zayden and Jonathan sit at the kitchen table, their plates filled with Hamburger Helper. They were in a suite in the woods in Maryland, waiting on everything to blow over with Scarlett. The cozy warmth of the kitchen light contrasted with the tension in the air. Jonathan tried to keep the atmosphere light for his son, but Zayden's quiet demeanor offered nothing but pushback.

"Is he okay?" Scarlett says as she spoke to him on the phone.

"Why don't you ask him yourself?" He removes the phone and extends it to Zayden, but he shakes his head no. Pressing the phone back against his drum he said, "He doesn't want to – ."

"Talk to me. I guess he's still mad. But he'll understand when I bring home his brother."

"For your sake, Scarlett, I hope so. Because once you ruin the bond between a mother and a son, it's gone forever."

"Don't you think I know that? That's what I'm fighting for!" She yells. "I'll be home soon."

When the call ends, he grabs his fork and plays with his food again. "You good, son?"

He looks up at him. "I hate her."

"Son don't ever say that! You don't know when or if you'll be able to take it back. Do you – ."

Suddenly, the front door burst open with a loud crash. Within moments, Bambi storms in, her presence commanding and fierce. Kevin followed closely behind, his eyes scanning the room for surprises or extra niggas. This was a married couple's affair as Bradley was at home, guarding Master, ensuring the young boy's safety. While Race and Denim were back at the spot waiting on Bambi to return. Let's just say it was a long night full of chaos.

The information that the stranger had given Bambi to follow out her plans had already proven to be reliable. As a result, Kevin was aimed and ready while Bambi placed a bottle of juice on the table. Then she removed her gun but kept it low.

Horrified, Jonathan jumped up from his seat and stood in front of his son when Zayden started crying, his small frame shaking with each sob. He looked at the juice and back at her. "What is this about?"

"I'm sure you know," Bambi says.

Zayden cries louder. "Son, you gonna be good," Jonathan said not really sure. "Right?" He looks at Bambi and Kevin who offer him no reprieve.

Not relieved, Zayden wouldn't let up on the hoopin' and hollerin'. Realizing his fear, Bambi's gaze softened slightly as she turned to the boy. After all, he was just a child.

"Shh, it's okay, Zayden. We're not here to hurt you," she said in a soothing tone." She winked. "As a matter of fact you got a brother you gonna get to meet when this is all said and done."

"That's a promise, young man," Kevin adds, his voice calm and reassuring.

Zayden wipes his tears away. "A brother? My mommy said I had one."

"It's true," she says. "Kevin, walk him into the room like the big man that he is."

Kevin nodded, took the boy's hand and strolled him in the other room in the suite.

Once alone, Bambi turns her attention to Jonathan, her eyes hardening. "You're a good-looking man, Jonathan," she says, her tone now cold and unyielding. "But I guess you wasn't fine enough to tame Scar. And for that you have to die."

"Please...all I want to do is be in his life. I never wanted her to hurt anybody."

"Too late."

Before Jonathan could react, Bambi raised her gun and fired. The shot echoed through the room, as his body fell to the floor, lifeless. When his blood poured at her feet, Bambi lowered her weapon, her expression unchanging.

Upon hearing the bullet, Kevin returns. "I'ma hang here with the kid," he said raising the juice. "Let me know when it's time to move." He walks up to her. "Before you go can I kiss you now?"

"If you gotta ask why bother?"

He grips her with one hand, and they kiss passionately, before she leaves out the door.

CHAPTER FORTY
THE MOMENT

A *small bell above the door chimed softly. Inside, red and gold were the dominant colors. If blood poured on the floor with a slight squint, you might miss it because it would blend in nicely. This made it the perfect location. As the beautiful criminals made entry, a young black couple, posted up doing nothing, looked their way.*

"I thought we had the whole place," Race said.

"We do," Bambi responded.

Bambi nodded at Race, issuing a silent order. Reading her mind, Race moved toward the couple, a flash of her gun shocking them as she dug into her pocket jacket, removing a wad of money instead of the handle of her gun.

They were lucky.

For now.

"It's like this...find someplace else to fucking eat."

"But we waiting on our ride," the woman said, scratching between the rows of her braids. She raised her strawberry shake to show her the frothy mess as if Race gave a fuck. "And I was sipping my drink. So nah, we good."

Thinking she got out on Race, her nigga chuckled...and then he saw something she didn't.

Danger.

Race leaned down. "If you don't get the fuck out of here, you gonna be sucking back blood." Now the weapon hung in her hand. "Is that drink that good?"

"We'll take the money."

Denim opened the door.

With five hundred dollars and their lives, they scurried out, the bell bidding them good fucking riddance.

With them gone, Bambi and her sisters slid into a corner red leather booth. Bambi sat alone on her side, while Denim and Race posted across from her. Nobody was comfortable but Bambi appeared confident as her eyes rested firmly on the door.

Shit felt heavy.

Like everything was on the line, because it was.

When Bambi's beautiful brown skin shimmered in the harsh white lights from the outside, Race nodded. "They here?"

Bambi nodded. "Get ready."

Within seconds, Scarlett pushed open the door to the diner, the bell above it chiming softly again. The place was deserted except for the back booth where they sat. Once inside, her arch enemies looked at her as if they never knew her.

Bambi, Race, and Denim, her former friends and sisters, now her adversaries wanted her blood. At one point she would have stood with them for the necessary, but now she was alone.

Frowning she said, "Where the fuck is my son, Bambi?"

"I see you by yourself," Denim said.

POW! POW! POW! POW! Gunshots rang in the distance, outside of the diner.

Race laughed. "Nah, but she by herself now."

Race knew that the men she hired to ambush the diner had murdered Scarlett's crew, because she set it up before even arriving. And since she had to make sure they were out of sight, she scanned the surroundings in the distance before even letting Bambi get out of the car. Only when Race was certain they were in position, did she allow her sisters to walk inside.

So what if her crew died.

Scarlett didn't care about them niggas. She wanted something else. "Where the fuck is my son, Bambi?" Scarlett demanded, her voice sharp. "And when will Master be turned over to me?"

Bambi exchanged a look with Race. "Let me make this clear. You never seeing Master in real life. As a matter of fact, you're never gonna have a life."

Bambi looked at Race and nodded. After getting the order, Race headed toward the door, with Scarlett watching her disappear, her heart pounding in her chest.

It seemed like forever but soon Race returned carrying a green duffle, a hamster in a cage, and an unmarked red drink in a soda bottle.

Scarlett knew the bottle and the liquid on sight. "You been in my...my house?"

Bambi sat back. "We used to talk a lot didn't we, Scarlett? Back when shit was good, and we loved each other. And I remember on those days when we were so fucked up, that you would reveal secrets to me no one else knew. Confessions of sorts."

Denim and Race were glued in also, neither hearing the story before.

"Like, I remember how you used to put your little girl asleep when she didn't want to go to bed." She raised the bottle. "With this drug induced red juice. But one time you gave her so much, she almost didn't wake up, causing her father to break your jaw in two places. That's when you learned that just a little bit..." she put two fingers together. "Just a little, will make her go to sleep. Whereas more, would make her stay asleep forever."

"You dirty, bitch!" Denim says to Scarlett. "How could you?!"

Bambi raised her hand to silence her. "You gave this to your baby? The new boy? You still got the same evil ways in your heart, girl?"

"I never laid a hand on my son. I was taking that shit! To get to sleep! To forget about the nightmares that plagued me way before meeting y'all!" She paused. "I would hurt myself whenever the urge hit." She opened her shirt revealing hundreds of raised scars on her chest from self-mutilation."

"Oh my God," Race said.

"Now where is this going, Bambi?" Scarlett said closing her shirt.

Bambi was momentarily taken off guard and for some reason felt more for Scarlett. But she fucked with her family so there was no going back. "You'll see," Bambi opened the cage and poured some of the red juice into the top of the soda bottle. She placed it in front of the animal and the hamster eagerly lapped it up.

"That's too much!" Scarlett said.

"I know. This is how you taught yourself dosages remember? Yeah, I remember all those conversations."

Next, she turned on a live video streamed from a closed network showing Kevin with Zayden. Alternating her looks between the video and her son, within seconds Scarlett watched in horror as the hamster dipped off into a permanent sleep. Now Scarlett saw the drink in from of Zayden and she wanted to throw up.

"That can happen to your son too, if you don't tell me what I want to know!"

"Please don't do this," Scarlett cried. "Please...I beg you."

"Fuck begging me! You sent a snake around my son!" Bambi opened the duffle Race carried and slammed a bloody scalp connected to a pink sew in on the table. It once belong to her friend. "When you know that's what the fuck we do to snakes!" Bambi pointed at it. "When you know how crazy I am!"

Having done the work, Race grins.

"Oh my...oh my God! You killed, Electra!" She covered her mouth with her hands.

"I know you had plans to hurt Melo. But I put a tracker on his car and found them both at that hotel. He's home and safe, while she's...well...dead. Now I want to know, who else has those videos?"

"Nobody! I swear!"

"Open your phone and show me the drive," Race said.

Scarlett fumbles with her phone but eventually pulls up the videos. Race deleted everything and changed the passcodes in case someone else had access. Everyone sat and waited until she was done.

"You got what you wanted, okay? Now please don't hurt Zayden!"

"Why the fuck should I care about your son?" Bambi pointed at the video of him and Kevin.

"Look at his eyes," Scarlett trembled.

"Fuck you talking about, whore?" Denim said.

"You plan every aspect of your life. Don't you, Bambi? You think you have an answer to it all." She laughed hysterically. "Well you couldn't plan this. So I want you to look at his fucking eyes!"

Bambi picked up the phone and zoomed in on Zayden's face. It took a moment but within seconds she saw what she wanted her to see. Confused and caught off guard, Bambi jumped up. "How...what...how?! What the fuck did you do, Scarlett?"

She sat back. "You know, that juice is good for more than just putting someone to sleep or killing them." She pointed to it. "The right drops will also sedate them. And one night...one night I sedated Melo when he was with Electra, and got pregnant by him because you know what? The dick stayed up!"

Race stole her in the face, followed by Denim.

Blood hung from the corner of her mouth, and she smiled.

"But Melo knows who you are!" Bambi yelled. "He once considered you an aunt and would have never touched you!"

"Not when he was high." She breathed deeply. "You may not care about my son, but do you got room in that cold ass heart for your grandson?"

Bambi wanted to faint. All her life she had an answer and now...now she was outplayed.

"The boy will be taken care of...because we real bitches. But that's more than I can say for you."

Race frowned and grabbed the phone and handed it to Denim. They see it too. He's Melo's son.

Bambi, Race, and Denim rise.

"Where y'all going?" Scarlett asked. "Where is my fucking son?!"

"Don't worry about all that," Bambi said with tears streaming down. "Someone else wants to talk to you first."

The Story Of The Stranger Known As
Samantha
Months Earlier

Samantha sat in her dimly lit room, the glow of her laptop screen casting eerie shadows on her face. The drone footage played on a loop, capturing every detail of the Kennedy King's compound from above.

As she worked with Vario, a hired drone operator, she gripped the edge of the desk, her knuckles white, her heart heavy with the weight of the past. She wanted just one sight of her mother because it was the last lead she knew. At first, she thought Scarlett, was still running with the Pretty Kings, and so she used the drones to track her down, hoping for a confrontation that would be long overdue on the property.

But things didn't go as planned and at first the Kennedy Kings lead ended in vain.

As Scarlett's first-born abandoned child, she had reason to hunt her down.

For as long as she could remember, memories of abuse flooded her mind. Nights spent in terror at the hands of her great-aunt and Scarlett's first aunt lived rent free in her heart. Whether cigarette burns, starving her, or verbal abuse, Samantha experienced it all from the same vile woman who tortured her mother.

Of course Samantha knew Scarlett suffered the same torment, but that knowledge didn't ease the pain. For real the anger festered with news of this issue, when she learned it from her racist uncle, who happened to be Scarlett's brother. As the years passed it pushed her to seek revenge against the woman who gave her life. She felt alone, forgotten by the one person who should have protected her, when the only man who loved her, her father, died.

By Scarlett's hand and that red juice poison.

Tracking Scarlett was a challenge.

She moved frequently, always slipping through Samantha's fingers. But after learning where the Kennedy's lived, after a lot of research and using their names within a digital footprint, she got lucky and needed a plant.

That's where the toy came in.

The bunny was the one dumb idea she didn't expect to work. But she figured that if at least the toy was in the house, she could see and hear what was happening through the bunny's eyes which also operated as a tracker.

Instead she was subject to sex acts between Bambi and Kevin before being splattered by paint by her brother, Master. Within time, the thing appeared to have a life of its own. Who would have thought that Master would take that toy with him to Bradley's car, and that Scarlett, as if drawn to it, would take it out of his vehicle and into her own house? Everyone was right to check it, but none thought about the eyes which on the surface looked like two golden buttons.

In a twist of fate her little brother would lead her to their mother and Bambi.

So that finally, after all this time, she would be able to confront her once and for all.

Now, standing in the secluded diner, Samantha finally had her chance. To ask the woman who gave her life why she hadn't fought harder to save her. Would it end her pain? Probably not, but she wanted to hear the words.

When the Pretty Kings left, Scarlett was about to leave when Samantha walked inside. Wondering who the rugged young woman was, Scarlett looked up, her eyes widening in surprise. "Samantha? Is that...is that you?"

"You know that it is." She extended her hand. "Sit."

She slowly took her seat. "Baby, what...what are you doing here?"

"That's not the real question." Samantha's voice trembled with emotion. "The real question is why did you abandon me?"

"I didn't abandon – ."

"You did! No one loved me after Dad died. All I experienced was hate and you never cared. I heard the conversations. How hard you were going for Master and even Zayden. But why fight for them and not me? Because that's what all of this was about right?"

Scarlett's eyes filled with tears. "Samantha, I'm so sorry. I never meant to leave you. Your father wouldn't allow me to see you and after that all I was doing was trying to survive. I had to let you go. But I...I never forgot what I did to you. What I put you through! Please...please forgive me!"

Samantha shook her head, her pain too deep to be soothed by apologies. "I needed you, and you weren't there. You should have protected me from her. Instead, you left me to suffer."

With her heart in shambles, Scarlett tried to reach across the table, but Samantha extended a trembling hand, stopping her.

"What can I do? There has to be something."

"There isn't."

Scarlett sits back, realizing her daughter meant her nothing but harm. "The bunny…was that you?"

"Yes."

"Why?"

"That woman, named Bunny, came to me a lot when I was younger. Asking around about you. Asked my daddy about you too. I didn't like or trust her, but I never forgot her name. She was the only connection I ever had to what you were really about. So I used the stuffed animal, a bunny, to plant my tracker."

"Sweetheart, what…what happens now?"

The room fell silent, the weight of Samantha's words hanging heavily in the air. As if it's a weight, she pulled a gun, her hands shaking as Scarlett's eyes widen in horror.

"If you gonna kill me, baby, please survive. Have a better life. Otherwise what you're about to do will be in vain. I even have an account set up for you when you turn twenty-five. Making you a wealthy woman."

"Ain't you listening? Everything I represent been in vain!" Tears stream down Samantha's face as she points the gun at her mother's heart. *"It's too late."*

With a single shot, she ends Scarlett's life. The sound echoes in the empty diner. As life exits her mother, Samantha stands there for a moment, the reality of what she has done sinking in. Knowing she had spent years to do this, she raises the gun and places it against her own heart, as tears flood her eyes altering her vision.

"Maybe now, we can be together forever, mama. Because I, I forgive you," she whispered, pulling the trigger once more.

As the echoes of the gunshots fade, Samantha's lifeless body falls beside her mother's, the two finally together in death.

CHAPTER FORTY-ONE
BAMBI

The night is dark, the road barely visible under the dim glow of the car's headlights. Denim is driving, gripping the steering wheel. The car is filled with a heavy silence, punctuated only by the occasional sniffle from Race sighing in the back seat.

I stare out the window, the events of the night replaying in my mind. Samantha killing Scarlett, in the diner haunts me, and I know we're all to blame.

Race shifts uncomfortably in her seat and finally breaks the silence. "Don't worry, Bambi. Zayden is your grandson, so we'll take care of him."

I turn to face her. "Of course, the baby will be fine," I reply, my voice steady. "But this is about us. Had we handled Scarlett better when we were friends, maybe this wouldn't have happened. And now we gotta carry this forever."

Denim glances over at me, her eyes filled with guilt and sadness. "Bambi, we did what we thought was right at the time."

"Nah, I could've handled it different," Race says. "She's right. This is all on me."

"This is on all of us. The fellas too." I shake my head, the weight of our actions pressing down on me. "Right or wrong, it doesn't matter now. We're all responsible in some way. And we have to live with that."

Race sighs, wiping a tear from her cheek. "What do we do now?"

I take a deep breath, trying to gather my thoughts. "We move forward. We protect Zayden and make sure he grows up safe. And we learn from this. We make sure we never let something like this happen again with us. No matter what Kevin and them do...the three of us have to remain tight."

"Agreed," Race says.

Denim looks at Race through the rearview mirror and replies, "Definitely."

EPILOGUE

*T*he Kennedy family arrived at the designated meeting spot, an old park on the outskirts of the city. As they approached the location, Master fidgeted nervously, clutching Bambi's hand. Kevin stood beside them, his expression tense but resolute. They were there to unite Master with his brother Zayden, facilitated by a case worker who verified that they were all related, something she had yet to reveal to Melo. The goal was simple, he would be living with the Kennedy Kings.

As they approached each other, the case worker stepped forward, eyeing Kevin and Bambi cautiously. "I'm not sure how comfortable he is," she said. "But after what happened to his mother being found how she was, he needs family."

Kevin nods solemnly. "We understand."

"He got that with us," Bambi said. "We just want what's best for the boys."

Zayden, stood beside the caseworker and looked at Master with curiosity. The two boys shared blood, which they will come to realize many years later.

Bambi knelt down beside Master. "This is your brother, Zayden. He's family."

Master nodded slowly, stepping forward to meet Zayden with an extended hand. The boys exchange a hesitant handshake, a small but significant step toward building a relationship.

As the adult's watch, the tension gradually disappeared, and it would have to. Because Zayden was a Kennedy, so he was stuck with them forever.

The church was beautifully decorated, filled with friends and family, including Race, Denim, Bradley, and Melo. In the center of it all, Bambi and Kevin stood at the altar, hands clasped, their faces radiant with joy. It was a new beginning, a chance to renew their vows and their commitment to each other.

This union began last week when Kevin took the first step to prove his devotion and willingness to let Bambi take the lead. He formally introduced her to Vidal Suarez, their cocaine distributor, especially since Suarez was no longer interested in looking for Mitch, who he supplied in the US.

But Bambi was taken aback when Kevin requested something in return. "You will no longer entertain Lucas."

Her stomach dropped. "How did you...how did you know?"

"I sent him to you, Bambi. When I knew you were looking. I vetted a man I knew would never try to take you from me. Because he knew how dangerous I could be. This is why he never spoke to you and only gave you what you felt you weren't getting from me."

"But how...why —"

"It doesn't matter. Just know that I already told him it's over," he said, interrupting her. "Can you handle it?"

She agreed, shocked and yet intrigued at how far he went.

And now it was their vow renewal day.

When it was time to proceed, the minister smiled warmly at them. "Do you, Kevin, take Bambi to be your lawfully wedded wife, to have and to hold, in sickness and in health, for better or for worse, till death do you part?"

Kevin gazed into Bambi's eyes, his voice steady and full of adoration. He wanted nothing more than to love her until his dying day and was grateful for another chance. He even participated in weekly counseling to heal what Bunny had done to his soul.

"I do," he said.

The minister turned to Bambi. "Do you, Bambi, take Kevin to be your lawfully wedded husband, to have and to hold, in sickness and in health, for better or for worse, till death do you part?"

Bambi's eyes glistened with tears of happiness. "I do."

"I now pronounce you man and wife!"

The church erupted, "Again!"

As they exchanged rings and sealed their vows with a kiss, the congregation exploded with applause. It was a moment of pure celebration, a promise of a brighter future.

Oddly enough, the pain that once plagued Bambi's body never happened again.

Later that evening, Race sat alone in her room, the weight of recent events heavy on her shoulders. There was a knock at the door. When she looked up she saw Bradley standing there.

"Can I come in?" He asked softly.

Race nodded, and he stepped inside, sitting beside her. "I'm sorry about everything, Race. I know you're hurting. With my brother and...just everything."

She sighed and leaned into his comforting presence. "It's just... a lot to process. Ramirez was still my person, despite everything else. And I hate to see how he went out."

"Can I hug you?"

She nodded and he wrapped his arms around her, holding her a little too long. Denim, passed by the door, saw their connection but chose to let it go.

For now anyway.

Eventually, Bradley pulled away. "I should go. Denim's waiting for me."

Race nodded and forced a smile. "Take care of her."

"I will. And I'll take care of you too," he knocked twice on the wall and left.

The grand opening of Kennedy Court was a momentous occasion, a celebration of resilience and hope. The Pretty Kings, alongside their husbands, The Kennedy Kings, despite their tumultuous past, gathered to reclaim their lives and looked forward to a brighter future.

The air was filled with music and laughter as the community came together to usher in a new era. Bambi and Kevin stood side by side with their son Melo, their bond stronger than ever. They chose to push the event back even further when Melo learned that Electra was murdered at the hotel when he went out to get

PRETTY KINGS 5   273

something to eat for them. Since it was a weird looking woman many thought it was connected to the assaults in the DMV area, and that the real target was Melo.

Of course he didn't know Bambi was involved. Still he needed to nurture his own heart and his family was there to care for him. This was only made worse when they had to bury Ramirez too.

Life was heavy but everyone was hopeful about the future.

As the evening continued, Denim and Bradley mingled with friends, enjoying the festivities. While Race was still grappling with her own emotions but finding solace in the company of her family.

Melo stood on the stage, looking out at the crowd. "This is a new beginning for all of us. And I'm proud to be doing it with family."

The crowd cheered, and the celebration continued, marking the start of a hopeful new chapter for the Kennedy family and Kennedy Court.

They didn't know it, but Suarez Vidal was also in attendance.

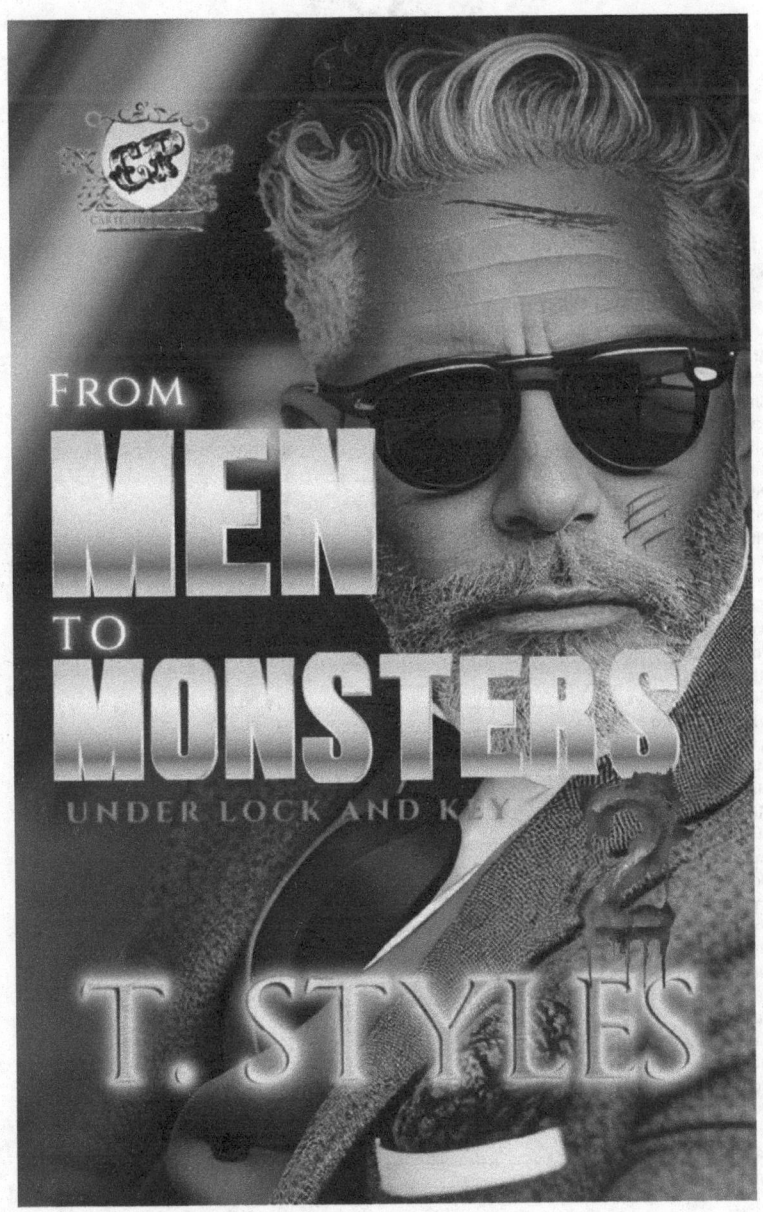

PRETTY KINGS 5

CARTEL PUBLICATIONS

PRESENTS

The Cartel Publications Order Form

www.thecartelpublications.com

Inmates **ONLY** receive novels for $14.00 per book **PLUS** shipping fee **PER BOOK.**

(Mail Order **MUST** come from inmate directly to receive discount)

Shyt List 1	_____	$15.00
Shyt List 2	_____	$15.00
Shyt List 3	_____	$15.00
Shyt List 4	_____	$15.00
Shyt List 5	_____	$15.00
Shyt List 6	_____	$15.00
Pitbulls In A Skirt	_____	$15.00
Pitbulls In A Skirt 2	_____	$15.00
Pitbulls In A Skirt 3	_____	$15.00
Pitbulls In A Skirt 4	_____	$15.00
Pitbulls In A Skirt 5	_____	$15.00
Victoria's Secret	_____	$15.00
Poison 1	_____	$15.00
Poison 2	_____	$15.00
Hell Razor Honeys	_____	$15.00
Hell Razor Honeys 2	_____	$15.00
A Hustler's Son	_____	$15.00
A Hustler's Son 2	_____	$15.00
Black and Ugly	_____	$15.00
Black and Ugly As Ever	_____	$15.00
Ms Wayne & The Queens of DC **(LGBTQ+)**	_____	$15.00
Black And The Ugliest	_____	$15.00
Year Of The Crackmom	_____	$15.00
Deadheads	_____	$15.00
The Face That Launched A Thousand Bullets	_____	$15.00
The Unusual Suspects	_____	$15.00
Paid In Blood	_____	$15.00
Raunchy	_____	$15.00
Raunchy 2	_____	$15.00
Raunchy 3	_____	$15.00
Mad Maxxx (4ᵗʰ Book Raunchy Series)	_____	$15.00
Quita's Dayscare Center	_____	$15.00
Quita's Dayscare Center 2	_____	$15.00
Pretty Kings	_____	$15.00
Pretty Kings 2	_____	$15.00
Pretty Kings 3	_____	$15.00

By T. STYLES

Pretty Kings 4	_____	$15.00
Silence Of The Nine	_____	$15.00
Silence Of The Nine 2	_____	$15.00
Silence Of The Nine 3	_____	$15.00
Prison Throne	_____	$15.00
Drunk & Hot Girls	_____	$15.00
Hersband Material **(LGBTQ+)**	_____	$15.00
The End: How To Write A _____		$15.00
Bestselling Novel In 30 Days (Non-Fiction Guide)		
Upscale Kittens	_____	$15.00
Wake & Bake Boys	_____	$15.00
Young & Dumb	_____	$15.00
Young & Dumb 2: Vyce's Getback	_____	$15.00
Tranny 911 **(LGBTQ+)**	_____	$15.00
Tranny 911: Dixie's Rise **(LGBTQ+)**	_____	$15.00
First Comes Love, Then Comes Murder	_____	$15.00
Luxury Tax	_____	$15.00
The Lying King	_____	$15.00
Crazy Kind Of Love	_____	$15.00
Goon	_____	$15.00
And They Call Me God	_____	$15.00
The Ungrateful Bastards	_____	$15.00
Lipstick Dom **(LGBTQ+)**	_____	$15.00
A School of Dolls **(LGBTQ+))**	_____	$15.00
Hoetic Justice	_____	$15.00
KALI: Raunchy Relived	_____	$15.00
(5ᵗʰ Book In Raunchy Series)		
Skeezers	_____	$15.00
Skeezers 2	_____	$15.00
You Kissed Me, Now I Own You	_____	$15.00
Nefarious	_____	$15.00
Redbone 3: The Rise of The Fold	_____	$15.00
The Fold (4ᵗʰ Redbone Book)	_____	$15.00
Clown Niggas	_____	$15.00
The One You Shouldn't Trust	_____	$15.00
The WHORE The Wind		
Blew My Way	_____	$15.00
She Brings The Worst Kind	_____	$15.00
The House That Crack Built	_____	$15.00
The House That Crack Built 2	_____	15.00
The House That Crack Built 3	_____	$15.00
The House That Crack Built 4	_____	$15.00
Level Up **(LGBTQ+)**	_____	$15.00
Villains: It's Savage Season	_____	$15.00
Gay For My Bae **(LGBTQ+)**	_____	$15.00
War		$15.00
War 2: All Hell Breaks Loose	_____	$15.00
War 3: The Land Of The Lou's	_____	$15.00
War 4: Skull Island	_____	$15.00
War 5: Karma	_____	$15.00
War 6: Envy	_____	$15.00
War 7: Pink Cotton	_____	$15.00
Madjesty vs. Jayden (Novella)	_____	$8.99
You Left Me No Choice	_____	$15.00
Truce – A War Saga (War 8)	_____	$15.00
Ask The Streets For Mercy	_____	$15.00

PRETTY KINGS 5

Truce 2 (War 9)	_____	$15.00
An Ace and Walid Very, Very Bad Christmas (War 10)	_____	$15.00
Truce 3 – The Sins of The Fathers (War 11)	_____	$15.00
Truce 4: The Finale (War 12)	_____	$15.00
Treason	_____	$20.00
Treason 2	_____	$20.00
Hersband Material 2 (LGBTQ+)	_____	$15.00
The Gods Of Everything Else (War 13)	_____	$15.00
The Gods Of Everything Else 2 (War 14)	_____	$15.00
Treason 3	_____	$15.99
An Ugly Girl's Diary	_____	$15.99
The Gods Of Everything Else 3 (War 15)	_____	$15.99
An Ugly Girl's Diary 2	_____	$19.99
King Dom (LGBTQ+)	_____	$19.99
The Gods Of Everything Else 4 (War 16)	_____	$19.99
Raunchy: The Monsters Who Raised Harmony	_____	$19.99
An Ugly Girl's Diary 3	_____	$19.99
From Men To Monsters (War 17)	_____	$19.99
Pretty Kings 5	_____	$19.99

(**Redbone 1 & 2** are **NOT** Cartel Publications novels and if **ordered** the cost is **FULL** price of **$16.00 each plus shipping. No Exceptions**.)

Please add **$8.00** for shipping and handling fees for up to **(2) BOOKS PER ORDER**. (INMATES INCLUDED) (See next page for details)

The Cartel Publications * P.O. BOX 486 OWINGS MILLS MD 21117

Name: _____

Address: _____

City/State: _____

Contact/Email: _____

Please allow 10-15 BUSINESS days Before shipping.

PLEASE NOTE DUE TO COVID-19 SOME ORDERS MAY TAKE UP TO 3 WEEKS OR LONGER BEFORE THEY SHIP

The Cartel Publications is NOT responsible for Prison Orders rejected!

NO RETURNS and NO REFUNDS
NO PERSONAL CHECKS ACCEPTED
STAMPS NO LONGER ACCEPTED

By T. STYLES